The Ground-Swell

The Ground-Swell

Mary Hallock Foote

Introduction by Maribel Morales

Hastings College Press | Hastings, Nebraska

Production Staff

Dakota Anderson

Emilie Barnes

Kaitlyn Baucom

Allie Belitz

Hannah Currey

Razvan Dobrin

Kaitlin Grode

Rachel Jesske

Alex Kreikemeier

Brooke MacLeod

Holly Wolfe

ISBN-10: 1942885040
ISBN-13: 978-1-942885-04-7

Note on the text: This edition has been reset from the first (1919) edition. Original spelling and grammatical conventions have been maintained, except in the case of publishing errors in the first edition. The original punctuation has been maintained but updated using modern conventions (e.g., eliminating spaces around dashes).

Manufactured in the United States of America

Contents

Introduction

Maribel Morales

Mary Anna Hallock Foote is a famous artist known for her illustrations and her novels and short stories set in the American West. Her designs embellished popular periodicals of the time as well as the works of writers such as John Greenleaf Whittier, Henry Wadsworth Longfellow, and Nathaniel Hawthorne. When she was only twenty years old she received her first commission to contribute illustrations for a book. As a woman this was an important accomplishment because "she was one of only a small number of women doing such serious work" (Bickford-Swarthout 1). She was one of the first American women to gain wide recognition as an illustrator, and in an overview of American "Women Illustrators" after the World's Columbian Exposition in Chicago in 1893 she was described as a "pioneer as an artist illustrator" (Morse 69).[1]

---

[1] The 1893 World's Columbian Exposition in Chicago included paintings and works by women artists and also samples of women's potential in the sciences and education. These works were presented inside the famous Woman's

Foote occupies a noteworthy position in American letters, publishing twelve novels and four volumes of short stories between 1880 and 1925. She also wrote an autobiography and numerous uncollected tales and sketches. However, as her biographer Lee Ann Johnson has pointed out, what makes Foote's literary production especially impressive is the fact that she not only dedicated herself to writing, but she also made the effort to illustrate her own stories (9). Her combined talents as author-illustrator "place her in a very select group whose union of graphic and verbal skills represents a special genius" (Johnson 9).

Early Literary Life

Mary Anna Hallock, who was called Molly, was born in 1847 to a Quaker family near Milton, New York, in the Hudson River valley. Her family had occupied a farm for five generations on the west side of the river, about seventy-five miles north of New York City. According to Christine Hill Smith, Hallock was born "at the right time and in the right place to take advantage of the cultural capital of her birth class and turn it into a moneymaking career" (*Social Class* 1). Hallock was talented and educated, and she was fortunate to have the support of her family in her aspirations to develop her artistic talent for drawing. She

---

Building, which was designed by Sophie Hayden, the first woman awarded a degree in architecture from the Massachusetts Institute of Technology. This project was a symbol that things were changing for women. Mrs. Potter Palmer, president of the women's committee for the exposition declared in her speech in the opening ceremony, "Even more important than the Discovery of Columbus, which we are gathered together to celebrate, is the fact that the general government has just discovered woman." In 1893, Alice C. Morse praised Foote's talent and her merit as a woman pioneer: "About twenty years ago, we could count on the fingers of one hand all the women seriously engaged in this work; not was it until the advent of Mrs. Mary Hallock Foote in the field, as the illustrator of her own charming stories, that illustration seemed to present an opening for women. Having obtained an entering wedge, they were not long in availing themselves of their opportunity" (68).

studied art in the School of Design for Women at the Cooper Union in New York City. She was almost seventeen when she began her studies in 1864. Here is where she met her best friend, Helena de Kay Gilder (1846–1916), who explained that the Cooper Union "was the only place, at that time, where anything approaching an art education could be had for a girl" (338). De Kay was an aspiring painter from Staten Island whose family belonged to elite cultural circles. The women came from different backgrounds but they remained very close friends throughout their lives. Helena de Kay married Richard Watson Gilder in 1874. He was editor of *Scribner's Monthly* and later of *The Century Magazine*. As Sue Rainey points out, Hallock's friendship with Helena de Kay and Richard Gilder "had a profound impact on her career" (102). They recognized her literary talent and encouraged her to write professionally.

After Mary Hallock's marriage in 1876 to Arthur de Wint Foote, a mining engineer from Connecticut, the couple went west. They were often apart, but she went with him to New Almaden, California; Leadville, Colorado; southern Idaho; and Grass Valley, California. Mary Hallock Foote was earning money with her illustrations; however, Helena and her husband Richard Gilder encouraged her to start writing after reading the letters Foote sent them describing the places she visited and the people she met. Richard Gilder's editorial policies encouraged regional literature and so he asked Foote to work some of her letters into articles for the magazine, providing a text for her illustrations of the West. Foote followed his advice and published two articles in *Scribner's*: "A California Mining Camp" in February 1878, about New Almaden, California, where her husband had his first post as a mining engineer in 1877; and "A Sea-Port on the Pacific" in August 1878, with descriptions of Santa Cruz, California, where she and their first child lived for part of a year. These two travel sketches of California proclaimed her debut as a writer. "A Sea-Port on the Pacific" brings up a theme that echoes throughout Foote's fiction: the differences between eastern and western society.

The favorable reception of her first novel, *The Led-Horse Claim* (1883), opened the way to other novels and short stories, which helped to support the Foote family financially, since Arthur's projects were not very successful. Mary Hallock Foote's list of unprecedented artistic and literary accomplishments is not complete without mentioning that she was also a wife and mother of three children, and she worked with her pen to support her family. Foote successfully pursued careers in two fields at a time when society expected women to live their lives in obedience to the emerging cult of domesticity and devote their lives to their roles as homemakers. The idea that women should remain in a separate sphere, centered on home and family, continued to prevail throughout the nineteenth and early twentieth centuries. Foote was able to juggle the roles of artist and mother, an experience she uses in her stories such as "The Fate of a Voice,"[2] where she presents Madeline, a young singer who struggles to balance her desire to be a professional singer and society's expectation for her to give up her dreams in order to marry an engineer and live in the West with him. Madeline represents Foote's ambivalent attitude towards the West, a place with beautiful landscapes, but lacking the literary and artistic circles Foote missed. In the end Madeline decides to follow society's expectations for her becoming a wife and following her husband: "She threw away a charming career, just at its outset, and went West with a husband—not anybody in particular. It was all-together a great pity" (Foote, *The Idaho Stories* 50). However, the voice was not completely lost because Madeline continued to sing in the West. As Darlis A. Miller concludes, in the final passage it is suggested that "an artist can have satisfaction in the West" (109): "The soul of music, wherever it is purely uttered, will find its listeners, though it be a voice singing in the wilderness, in the dawn of the day of art and beauty which is coming to a new country and a new people" (Foote, *The Idaho Stories* 50).

---

[2]   "The Fate of a Voice" was first published in 1889 and later was included in the 1988 collection of stories *The Idaho Stories and Far West Illustrations of Mary Hallock Foote* edited by Barbara Cragg, Dennis M. Walsh, and Mary Ellen Walsh.

Foote draws from a wide variety of her personal life experiences as both author and illustrator. Therefore, as Lee Ann Johnson explains, her literary works "are best analyzed within their biographical context" (9). She provides the nation a view of the American West different from anything offered by male artists and writers. Darlis A. Miller explains that Foote was "one of the first and most articulate women to write about the West and was the first to write about mining camps from first-hand knowledge" (xiii). As a result, scholars have highlighted the authenticity of her fiction, "generated by the perception and depiction of a mythical West other than that popularized by mainstream western critics and authors—an inner reality with all its attendant ambiguities" (Armitage 164).

When Mary Hallock Foote left Boise in 1895 she had become the first writer and illustrator to publish a substantial amount of work set in Idaho. As her novels, stories, essays, and illustrations appeared in *Century Magazine, The Atlantic Monthly,* and *St. Nicholas Magazine* (a magazine for children), Foote introduced a large national audience to the new West that she had found. Foote was a sensitive eastern lady of the Victorian era who was simultaneously wife and mother, novelist and artist in the Far West. She experienced a continuous tension between her enthusiasm for the West's natural beauty and the yearning for the intellectual and social stimulation of the literary and artistic world of New York City. Melody Graulich explains that Foote "is a paradoxical Westerner, claiming when she first went West, 'I never felt so *free* in my life'" ("Western Biodiversity" 50). The adjustment from the social standards of the eastern upper class to the western way of life was a challenge for her. She published her Idaho stories in *Century Magazine* at a time when the Foote family was undergoing many personal problems.

Regional Literature

Although Mary Hallock Foote was successful at balancing a career with her home life, this was still a challenge for nineteenth-century women in general. Women writers felt a double oppression: as women they were expected to be the guardians of their homes as mothers and wives, since the public sphere was controlled by men; as writers, they were secluded from the main intellectual literary centers, also dominated by men. Coincidentally, at the very time that American literature was beginning to be defined, it denigrated women's contributions to it. However, writers in various parts of the country were developing a genre of which women would be major practitioners. It was first called "local color" literature because of its representations of the language, customs, geography, and manners of specific regions. Scholars in recent years have preferred the term "regional literature."

This genre consists primarily of short stories and sketches that capture the flavor of ordinary lives in New England, the West, the South, and, to a lesser extent, the Midwest. Thus, regionalist literature offered women writers a literary space where they could develop their stories and have their own literary voice. The literary regionalism of the West bloomed in the 1870s and 1880s. Although the most notorious regionalist writers of the West are Bret Harte and Mark Twain, there were many women writing fiction about the West, including Gertrude Atherton, Alice Cary, Mary Hunter Austin, Helen Hunt Jackson, Carolina Kirkland, and Mary Hallock Foote.[3] Regionalism was considered appropriate for women at the beginning of the nineteenth century because it was perceived as a "minor" genre, thus inferior.

Foote's desperate need to write to support her family while her husband was without a salary made her write conventional stories with the expected happy ending. In spite of this, Foote did write some stories during this period that showed some promise

---

[3] By the 1870s and 1880s, writers such as Sarah Orne Jewett and Mary Wilkins Freeman were writing stories about New England, Mary Hunter Austin was exploring the desert in California and Arizona, Mary Hallock Foote was experiencing the mining region of Idaho, and Kate Chopin was writing about New Orleans and particularly about strong complex female characters. As part of the development of literary realism in the second half of the nineteenth century, this fiction features particularly strong delineations of characters, especially women.

and are indicative of what she might have written if she had been free of the conventions of the time. However, as Rodman W. Paul writes in *A Victorian Gentlewoman in the Far West*, "even if she had mixed feelings about life out there, nevertheless she learned to write about it and draw it, and thereby to reach an audience of thousands of easterners" (v). During this time she was a popular regionalist writer well known in the literary field, as well as a famous illustrator.

The Ground-Swell and the New Woman

In her last novel, *The Ground-Swell* (1919), Foote presents the theme of the New Woman and the impact it has on a traditional family. The narrator has a conservative view on the expectations of women and is forced to see the emergence of feminism in her own family with her unconventional daughter. Foote presents a mother debating herself about tradition and the positive aspects of being a modern woman. In the novel, Katherine represents the New Woman—she is a member of the so-called "third sex"[4]—and her mother represents the social

---

[4]   The term "third sex" has a long history. Gilbert Herdt in *Third Sex, Third Gender: Beyond Sexual Dimorphism in Culture and History* (1994) explains that the term has changed since the third century to its more modern use in the eighteenth-century to describe homosexual men and some women (10). Toward the end of the nineteenth century and beginning of the twentieth century, the "third sex" was used to describe homosexuality with negative connotations. The term was used in moderation until the emergence of "queer theory," which gave it a new meaning. In sociological books such as Patricia A. McBroom's *Third Sex: The New Professional Woman* (1986), the term does not have homosexual connotations; instead it represents American women who succeeded in masculine professions. At the time Mary Hallock Foote wrote *The Ground-Swell* (1919), the term "third sex" did not always refer to lesbians, but it is possible that it had certain connotations. In spite of the history of homosexuality surrounding the origin of the term "third sex," the expression has been generally considered as a reference to a person who does not follow the conventional roles of sexuality. This interpretation is perhaps the most accurate in Foote's novel since there are no references to Katherine being a lesbian. According to Christine Hill Smith, Katherine is "clearly heterosexual" (*Social Class* 133).

resistance against these women. In the 1890s and early twentieth century, women were starting to refuse marriage or postpone it, and instead they pursued a professional career and working outside their home. In the novel, Foote presents a group of New Women: college-educated women who are independent, living alone or with other women.

The novel is narrated from the point of view of Lucy Cope, Katherine's mother, and "the first-person narrative takes the form of the mother's correspondence to her closest friend" (Johnson 146). The novel also presents a realistic portrayal of a mother's anxieties about her children: a mother concerned with the happiness of her daughters. Darlis A. Miller argues that in four of Foote's novels written early in the twentieth century, she created "a handful of memorable older women protagonists," Lucy Cope being one of such strong personalities that "linger in the reader's memory long after the books are put aside" (253). According to Miller, the novel benefits from "having an older woman author explore themes of such universal appeal as parent-child relations and family tragedy and triumphs" (253). Foote sets her novel in the beginning of the twentieth century; however, the themes are still relevant today as she explores the struggles of parenthood and the relationship of parents with their children as they are growing up. Her personal experiences and her treatment of these universal themes make this story authentic in its representation of life in the early twentieth-century.

Foote wrote other novels in which she explored the relationships between parents and their children, but in *The Ground-Swell* she used her own daughter Agnes as inspiration for the character of Katherine, and in doing so she immortalized her memory. Agnes died in 1904 from appendicitis when she was only seventeen years old. Before her death, Foote had managed to write at least one short story every couple of months, even during difficult times, but this tragedy affected her so deeply that she was unable to write for six years. Foote probably drew from another real woman as well, a sister of her husband. Lee Ann Johnson argues that the character of Katherine derives in part from "Arthur's sister Katherine, who had insisted she was 'not a marrying woman' and had followed a successful career in New York; but primarily she is Agnes" (148). In the novel, Katherine is twenty-seven years old, and she is part of a group of women who decide not to get married or have children, but instead they dedicate their lives to helping others as social workers. Katherine's mother cannot understand her daughter's ideas and decisions. The choice of the family last name anticipates the suffering this mother has to "cope" with in order to accept the changes in society, and particularly how that affects her own family.

The book was published in 1919 when the Nineteenth Amendment was ratified and women lost the opportunity to win the right to vote. Foote did not support women's suffrage because it was against her beliefs as a Quaker. Her friends Helena and Richard Gilder also influenced her. As an editor, Richard had published numerous articles against women's suffrage. Christine Hill Smith argues that from reading Foote's autobiography and letters it can be argued, "she did not approve of women's political independence on many fronts" (*Social Class* 118). Despite Foote's beliefs, she presents her readers with "a glimpse of a thriving female community living and working in New York City in the 1910s" (Smith, *Social Class* 118). Not all New Women were involved in politics, though the suffragettes were considered New Women. They were the first women to receive a college education, becoming the first female doctors, lawyers, public officials, and businesswomen in the industrialized world. Christine Hill Smith argues that although Foote wrote about the New Woman, she produced a "polite version of such groundbreaking circumstances," ignoring certain aspects of these independent women and creating for her characters a refined world "that suited her own comfort level" (*Social Class* 118).

The Ground-Swell opens in California in the summer of 1914, one year before World War I, and it was inspired by the Footes' summer of 1915, when they vacationed at Pescadero Point, south of San Francisco. For Lucy Cope and her husband Charles, a retired general in the army, "a summer camping vacation along the northern California shoreline becomes the occasion for introspection and discovery" (Johnson 146). The

Copes search for a good place for their last home as they vacation in Laguna Point, where they hope Katherine will also live. Lee Ann Johnson explains that Lucy and Charles Cope come to realize that "the ground swells they watch—the deep ocean swells occasioned by disturbances far out at sea—symbolize the disorder within and without their coastal world" (146). The disorder they experience comes mainly from the lives of their daughters; as James Maguire states, the "old-age idyl of the Copes is disrupted by the ground-swell of emotions reaching them from their daughters' lives," particularly the two oldest, Cecily and Katherine (41). Katherine's sisters, Patty and Cecily, are married. Patty is stationed with her army husband in the Philippines, and Cecily marries a wealthy San Francisco playboy who eventually deserts her when she is pregnant. The Copes are unable to help Cecily ease her agony, and Mrs. Cope also fails in her plan to find a suitor for Katherine. Her mother thinks that if she finds a suitor for her daughter she might convince her to get married. When Katherine visits her parents at Laguna Point, her mother introduces her to Tony Kayding, caretaker of the place where they are camping. However, the young man is firmly rejected since Katherine prefers to be dead than married: "As for marrying him, I'd as soon he swam out to sea with me and we drowned out there together in the sunset" (119). James Maguire points out that "the old mother realizes that the new generation will not be molded by every parental whim, but she also knows how much influence she does have, and she tries to use that to good effect" (43). Unfortunately, the parental influence can do only so much to guide their daughters, and this is what makes this novel so relevant to any time period.

Even though Mrs. Cope's experiment to bring Katherine and Tony together fails, Katherine did develop some feelings for Tony. One of Katherine's aspirations is to build a big school to educate women and train them in a profession. In that school there would be teachers "of all kinds and all sexes, even the 'third sex'" (105). This school would provide "everything in work or play that can make a girl fit and manly" (105). These plans are shocking for her young suitor, who is particularly surprised by the word "manly", so Katherine further explains, "I would have my daughters to be valiant and brave men" (106). Through the character of Mrs. Cope, Foote presents the conflicting emotions that mothers of this time might have experienced when trying to accept the choices of their modern daughters. Christine Hill Smith adds, "for selfish reasons, Mrs. Cope wants Katherine near her, preferably married" ("Reading" 120), but marriage was not in Katherine's plans. She "had joined herself to books and to women of advanced ideas" and for that reason her mother was afraid that her ideas "would end in a complete revolt against the old order" (43). The ideals of modern women seemed like a threat to the values that society believed in for decades.

From the very beginning Mrs. Cope believes that her daughter Katherine "was our disappointment" (22) because when she was born they were expecting a boy. Katherine behaves like a boy from childhood, and when they live in the military base, she imitates the soldiers during their training. She is difficult to describe physically, although she possesses a special charm: "Her strange little face, that no portrait has preserved, so unregular, unpretty, but so fascinating" (57). Katherine dresses in a masculine way, which makes her mother insist that she wear more feminine clothes. Mrs. Cope also dislikes the fact that her daughter smokes. She sees that she is "a boy in her attitudes and as careless of pose" but she loves her because she "was the offspring of our hearts' blood." Katherine is her "wild star" but she is also her "darling" (110). Despite her boyish manners, Mrs. Cope describes her daughter as "our pride because of how she had turned out" but again she cannot help to feel that Katherine is also "in some ways our despair" (22). In her *Reminiscences* Mary Hallock Foote wrote that when Agnes was born she thought, "in our certain way of life we needed another boy rather than another girl" (301). Like Mrs. Cope, Foote had hoped for a boy because "even in our family, where all the women were self-supporting, that old tradition still held; that boys are sure to be an asset and girls a liability" (*Reminiscences* 301).

Lucy and Charles Cope spend the winter in New York where they meet Katherine's friends. Katherine's experience living in New York City recalls Mary Hallock Foote's life as a young art student. Christine Hill Smith explains that Katherine doing social work in New York City "has the same excitement for life that Foote herself had for that city over forty years earlier" and that she used her own memories of "independent youth" in this character ("Reading" 27). Lucy is perplexed by the behavior of Katherine's friends, however. Just like a man, Katherine is independent and lives in an apartment in New York with another woman, Sarah Huntwell. Sarah refers to Katherine as her "wife," something that to Mr. and Mrs. Cope "struck as 'new'" (189). Later on Mrs. Cope herself refers to Sarah as "Katherine's husband" (175), showing a small step toward accepting the New Women's lifestyle. The two women shared the household duties; they "kept their mutual accounts and paid the bills in a manly fashion" (152). These characteristics describe the so-called "Boston marriage," a term that was used at the end of the nineteenth century in New England to describe a monogamous relationship between two single women. These women generally did not depend economically on a man; they earned their own money working or they inherited money. Another characteristic of the Boston marriage is that the majority of these women were feminists, women who were very involved in social and cultural improvement. Katherine works at "the Wiser Mothers and Better Babies" and she firmly defends the work she does to help other women and their children: "If one woman in the course of her working life could help, say, one hundred other women to feed their babies better, so half of them wouldn't die and the other half grow up deficient in some way—there you'd have an average of three or four hundred better Americans to three or four the one woman might produce if she went in for babies of her own. Isn't it good economics?" (157). But Mrs. Cope does not agree with her daughter.

Although Foote is going against her values by presenting a modern woman, she does not criticize this group of women. Instead she offers a sympathetic view. Foote, like Mrs. Cope, is making an effort to adapt to the new tendencies. Mrs. Cope is invited to a "third-sex dinner" (173) where all guests are women.

Here she can see how intelligent and educated these modern women are, but she is not capable of accepting their ideals or even understanding them. To her these women speak another language: "Charley and I did not speak the language of these wonderful, super-civilized young goddesses which our latest times have evolved. Looking at them in their intelligence and grace and power, and the self-confidence that perfect form, manner, social background gives, their superb health and in some cases beauty … it made me long to swear! … 'The ungrateful hussies, they will not marry!'" (173). Mrs. Cope feels a mixture of admiration and frustration seeing these women stick to their modern ideas. Seeing these women smoking together after dinner, Mr. and Mrs. Cope are thankful they are not part of this new generation: "Privately, Charley and I thanked our stars we were born before this deluge" (175).

Renewed Reputation

After living more than fifty years in the West, Mary Hallock Foote and her husband moved back east to retire. Mary died at the age of ninety in 1938. The artwork and writing she left behind provide us with an important record of an eastern woman's life in the West. After a period of relative oblivion, Foote has recently received considerable attention for her novels and short stories. References about Mary Hallock Foote's literary career are scarce until the 1980s[5] when there is a renewed interest in her. The Idaho State University Press published the first collection of her stories in 1988 with the title *Idaho Stories and Far West Illustrations of Mary Hallock Foote*. Until this moment, Foote's short stories from her time in Idaho had not been republished, and thanks to this collection, her stories

---

[5]   In 1971, Wallace Stegner wrote *Angle of Repose*, a novel inspired by the life of Mary Hallock Foote. This novel called the attention of Foote's scholars, who criticized Stegner's book for plagiarizing fragments of the story that were written by Foote herself. As a result of this controversy, numerous essays were published analyzing the novel and its connections to Foote.

became accessible to a larger audience, stimulating the interest of readers and critics. From the 1990s to the present time, multiple articles have been published about Foote in books about Western American writers. Articles about Foote can also be found in books about ecocriticism, which shows an increase in the interest of feminist criticism and gender geography. Her stories are also published in anthologies not only about Western literature but in collections that showcase her talent among nineteenth-century American women writers.[6] Evaluations of Mary Hallock Foote's fiction by 21st-century scholars are varied. New biographies have been published as well as new essays and a book analyzing Foote's fiction. The number of publications about Foote has increased, and, although she is still better known in the Western United States as a Western regionalist writer, her talent as author and illustrator deserve to be recognized at a national level.

Works Cited

Armitage, Shelley. "The Illustrator as Writer: Mary Hallock Foote and the Myth of the West." *Under the Sun: Myth and Realism in Western American Literature.* Ed. Barbara Howard Meldrum. Troy, New York: The Whiston Publishing Company, 1985.

Baym, Nina. *Women Writers of the American West, 1833–1927.* Urbana, Chicago and Springfield: University of Illinois Press, 2011.

Bickford-Swarthout, Doris. *Mary Hallock Foote: Pioneer Woman Illustrator.* Deansboro, NY: Berry Hill, 1996.

Floyd, Janet. "A Sympathetic Misunderstanding? Mary Hallock Foote's Mining West." *A Journal of Women's Studies,* 22. 3, (2001): 148–167.

---

[6]   Mary Hallock Foote's stories and sketches: "The Fate of a Voice," "Looking for Camp," "The Coming of Winter," and "The Sheriff's Posse" are included in Karen L. Kilcup's *Nineteenth-Century American Women Writers: An Anthology,* 1997.

————. "Mining the West: Bret Harte and Mary Hallock Foote." *Soft Canons: American Women Writers and Masculine Tradition.* Iowa City: University of Iowa Press, 1999.

Foote, Mary Hallock. *A Victorian Gentlewoman in the Far West, the Reminiscences of Mary Hallock Foote.* Ed. Introduction by Rodman W. Paul. San Marino, CA: Huntington Library, 1972.

————. *The Idaho Stories and Far West Illustrations of Mary Hallock Foote.* Ed. Barbara Cragg, Dennis M. Walsh and Mary Ellen Walsh. Pocatello: Idaho State University Press, 1988.

Graulich, Melody. "Legacy Profile: Mary Hallock Foote, 1847–1938." *Legacy: A Journal of Nineteenth-Century American Women Writers 3*, 2 (Fall 1986): 43–52.

————. "Western Biodiversity: Rereading Nineteenth-Century American Women's Writing." Ed. Karen L. Kilcup. *Nineteenth-Century American Women Writers: A Critical Reader.* Blackwell Publishers, 1998. 47–61.

Herdt, Gilbert. *Third Sex, Third Gender: Beyond Sexual Dimorphism in Culture and History.* New York: Zone Books, 1994.

Johnson, Lee Ann. *Mary Hallock Foote.* Boston: Twayne Publishers, 1980.

Kay Gilder, Helena de. "Mary Hallock Foote." *The Book Buyer,* 11 (August 1894): 338.

Kilcup, Karen L. *Nineteenth-Century American Women Writers: An Anthology.* Blackwell Publishing, 1997.

Maguire, James H. "Mary Hallock Foote." *Boise State College Western Writers Series 2.* Boise: Boise State College Press, 1972.

McBroom, Patricia A. *The Third Sex: The New Professional Woman.* New York: Morrow, 1986.

Miller, Darlis A. *Mary Hallock Foote: Author-Illustrator of the American West.* Norman: University of Oklahoma Press, 2002.

Morse, Alice C. "Women Illustrator." *Art and Handicraft in The Woman's Building of the World's Columbian Exposition.* Ed. Maud Howe Elliott. Chicago: Rand McNally, 1893.

Rainey, Sue. "Mary Hallock Foote: A Leading Illustrator of the 1870s and 1880s." *Winterthur Portfolio,* 41. 2/3 (Summer/ Autumn 2007): 97–140.

Shein, Debra. "When Geography Matters: Mary Hallock Foote's <Maverick> and the Mysteries of the Snake River Lava Beds." *American Literary Realism,* 38. 3 (Spring 2006): 249–258.

Smith, Christine Hill. "Reading A Victorian Gentlewoman in the Far West: The Reminiscences of Mary Hallock Foote." *Boise State University Western Writers Series* No. 154, 2002.

———. *Social Class in the Writings of Mary Hallock Foote.* Reno & Las Vegas: University of Nevada Press, 2009.

Other Works by Mary Hallock Foote

Novels

The Led-Horse Claim: A Romance of a Mining Camp. Boston: James R. Osgood and Company, 1883.

John Bodewin's Testimony. Boston: Ticknor and Company, 1886.

The Last Assembly Ball, and the Fate of a Voice. Boston: Houghton, Mifflin, and Company, 1889.

The Chosen Valley. Boston and New York: Houghton, Mifflin, and Company, 1892.

Coeur d'Alene. Boston: Houghton, Mifflin, and Company, 1894.

The Prodigal. Boston and New York: Houghton, Mifflin, and Company, 1900.

The Desert and the Sown. Boston: Houghton, Mifflin, and Company, 1902.

The Royal Americans. Boston: Houghton, Mifflin, and Company, 1910.

A Picked Company. Boston and New York: Houghton, Mifflin,
     and Company, 1912.
The Valley Road. Boston and New York: Houghton, Mifflin, and
     Company, 1915.
Edith Bonham. Boston and New York: Houghton, Mifflin, and
     Company, 1917.
The Ground-Swell. Boston and New York: Houghton, Mifflin,
     and Company, 1919.

Collections of Stories

In Exile and Other Stories. Boston and New York: Houghton,
     Mifflin, and Company, 1894.
The Cup of Trembling, and Other Stories. Boston: Houghton,
     Mifflin, and Company, 1895.
The Little Fig-Tree Stories. Boston: Houghton, Mifflin, and
     Company, 1899.
A Touch of Sun and Other Stories. Boston: Houghton, Mifflin, and
     Company, 1903.
The Idaho Stories and Far West Illustrations of Mary Hallock Foote.
     Eds. Barbara Cragg, Dennis M. Walsh and Mary Ellen
     Walsh. Pocatello: Idaho State University Press, 1988.

Autobiography

*A Victorian Gentlewoman in the Far West: The Reminiscences of
     Mary Hallock Foote.* Ed. Rodman Paul. San Marino, CA:
     Huntington Library, 1972.

Further Reading

Blend, Benay. "A Victorian Gentlewoman in the Rocky
     Mountain West: Ambiguity in the Work of Mary Hallock
     Foote." *Reading Under the Sign of Nature: New Essays in
     Ecocriticism.* Ed. John Tallmadge and Henry Harrington.
     Salt Lake City: University of Utah Press, 2000.
Floyd, Janet. "Mining the West: Bret Harte and Mary Hallock
     Foote." *Soft Canons: American Women Writers and Masculine*

Tradition. Ed. Karen K. Kilcup. Iowa City: University of
   Iowa Press, 1999.
Rodman, Paul. *When Culture Came to Boise: Mary Hallock Foote
   in Idaho.* Boise: Idaho State Historical Society, 1977.

....

Maribel Morales is Assistant Professor at Carthage College,
Wisconsin, where she teaches courses in American Literature
and Spanish. She completed her PhD in American Literature in
2010 from the University of Cádiz, Spain, where she is from. Her
scholarship includes gender and ethnic studies in nineteenth- and
early twentieth-century American women writers. In the United
States, she presented her latest research at the Willa Cather
Spring Conference, as well as at other conferences organized by
the American Literature Association and the Western Literature
Association among others. She recently published an article on
ecofeminism in the works of Willa Cather, Sarah Orne Jewett,
Mary Austin, and Kate Chopin in the *Willa Cather Newsletter
and Review.*

I

We were at our last post in the Philippines when
my husband, then colonel of the —th Cavalry, reached
the age limit for the army and was retired with the
rank of brigadier general, after forty-two years' service;
and we thought, my soldier-man and I, that we were
done for the rest of our lives with bugle-calls and long
envelopes from headquarters.

He had been given four months' leave in advance
of the date (of his retiracy), which covered our journey
home and a little time thereafter for him to look
about him and consider the changes one expects to
find after a three years' exile, before deciding on what
he should do with his left-over years. A man neither
young nor old—no longer keen for the adventure of
some new occupation nor old enough to live without
any—can scarcely face those years and not feel a certain
blankness, a sense of having been stripped of more than

his soldier-clothes, of having lost, indeed, a large part of his identity.

For us, with three daughters in as many different quarters of the globe, any move of ours brought us nearer to one and farther from another; this time we were leaving Patty, our youngest, in the Philippines, a bride of ten weeks, and closing the distance to Katherine in New York and Cecily in San Francisco whom we had not seen in three years. We could barely say we were acquainted with our new son-in-law aside from his record as an officer; still, we did not disapprove of Patty's young venture: Patty's own mother had married a first lieutenant whom her parents had taken on trust, and followed the flag with him thirty-three years as he went up the grades. The little son we lost, our first baby, born in Arizona, would have been thirty-two that spring.

In February, we landed in San Francisco, which has been called the mother-in-law of the army for the number of army brides the city has supplied from its uncommonly attractive daughters. It had given us a son-in-law, some years before while we were stationed at the Presidio. We stayed at the son-in-law's house and visited our eldest daughter, Cecily. And from there we moved into temporary quarters in Berkeley for what time we expected to give to considering our further plans for the summer.

We knew ourselves provincial,—the American Army is, compared to the British in its garrisons all over the world,—but we thought we were not unadaptable. We had packed and unpacked our modest possessions ("plunder," as we call it in the army) in about every post where the old flag is raised. As a soldier's wife I was expected to fit my family's curves into the holes and corners of any house or hut the Government provided; it could not be said we were pampered. We had gathered some moss of sentiment in each place where we had been happy and we were happy in most places. But all along we had dreamed and talked of the home that some day should be permanent. There are certain kinds of moss it is useless to gather unless you have got somewhere to keep it; books we had never dared to buy because their weight eats up one's transportation allowance, and we never had dug ourselves in very deep in the matter of gardens.

"And now," my colonel vaunted—he will still be "colonel" to me; "general" I hated, in a way, because it was his old-age rank and put him on the retired list (with a larger pension, of course, which no one undervalues in the army)—"And now we'll show 'em a garden! It will be your garden, but I expect to do most of the work in it; and it will not be in a hot climate if I know it." He admitted we must have sun enough to make things grow and not too much frost in winter, a winter that would spare tea roses and daphne, and a soil that would not ruin us in fertilizers.

With these specifications in mind, and one other which I leave till later, we planned our summer pilgrimage in search of some spot we could afford to

buy on which to build our house with its modest book-
room and lay out the first real garden of our whole
lives. We did not propose to waste any of that house
and garden money on Peninsular hotels, and we were
not wedded to Scenic Drives and Highways: "old roads
winding as old roads will" should tempt us provided
they wound in the right direction; nor did we stop
to consider any of the pretty suburbs and "residential
districts" suggested by friends whose tastes were as good
as our own. It was room we wanted, and a chance for
a little solitude (*à deux,* of course) which army people
never have. But we knew that at our age we could not
afford to despise comfort. No roadside fires for me, a
grandmother, nor sod of San Mateo County, however
rich, for my husband's good gray head.

In March, by means of catalogues from a sporting-
goods house in New York, he collected his camp outfit
meticulously to his mind; about the same time he
bought a five passenger car. In April he had a "trailer"
built in a wagon-shop in Oakland under his very
eye. And the Lord sent us Harvey. I scarcely expect
to be believed, yet it is true that for this trip at least
Harvey, who, though not in the uniformed class, is
an experienced chauffeur and can doctor his own car,
consented likewise to be packer and wood-chopper
and water-carrier and dish-washer and assistant cook
(my husband was chef)—and all without knowing
how he would be treated, so to speak. Army officers
have a reputation for what is sometimes considered
when looked at personally as snobbishness. I shall not

pretend that Charley's tact may not have had a good deal to do with our triumph in this matter. He would not be fit for a woman to camp with, of course, if he had not enough of it to know how to treat a good American like Harvey.

With one delay and another it was mid-July when we crossed the Oakland ferry with our trailer behind us, ordered about by deck-officers and glared at by teamsters not prepared for the length-of-us and all mixed up in turning. We got ourselves off the boat and drove up Market Street and out Valencia and Mission—the stream of flashing cars we met from Burlingame and San Mateo might have held some of the people we had dined with when we were staying with Cecily; they glanced at us in a distant, well-bred way that took in our tent-poles and other vagaries. We were of a different world already, the family of trailers. Business trailers may have been common enough, but at that time, the summer of 1914, I had never seen a domestic trailer built to order like our own. Occasionally I looked back to see what it was doing. It waddled along on a pair of soundless automobile-tires, its hump-back covered with a tarpaulin roped down to hooks on its sides, giving it the appearance of something between a haystack and a baby elephant as it followed the mother-car. Charley had been annoyed at my pessimism when he first proposed this mode of travel. Had he ever built a trailer before? Wouldn't the attachment he called a "coupling" spoil the smartness of our new Buick? Wouldn't that short tongue that looked like a snout (or the elephant-child's trunk before it was pulled out) horn us or nose us off the road on some sharp curve, or contrive our destruction in some way? I had been accustomed to take the route from my husband as he took his orders; but on this trailer-trip he was no better than an amateur in my eyes and I had allowed him to see it. And he might have recriminated now, but he was much too content.

He does not ask me if he may smoke—he always smokes, when we ride in silence mile after mile. That is one reason why he hates to drive his own car. On his stout knee lay spread open one of the Coast Survey charts (cut in squares and backed with linen for folding); the arch of his nose in profile under the brim of his tweed traveling-cap, his gray mustache, cigar, and heavy chin were between me and the landscape; and because Cecily is his own child in good looks, though with every feature softened and perhaps weakened a little, I began to think about her, the daughter we had seen last, and known so little about during those years in the Philippines. Her letters had not been at all revealing. We could only guess how that marriage had turned out, and after two weeks in her house we were still guessing—about some things; others we knew.

Cecily was the daughter whose life to all appearances seemed almost inflatedly happy, yet whose securities in life we tacitly put least faith in. And since we could not be near all three of our daughters, Cecily was the one who, we thought, might some day need us most. Not in material ways; secure would have been a ridiculous word for the circumstances her choice of a husband had placed her in.

We were swinging down the long grades of the Santa Cruz road nearing the little town of Vallevista, the sky pearly with lingering fog on the sea-view side, and deep, far blue over the mountains or hills on our left; the road smooth as a floor and clean as if swept by winds from off the ocean; that day it was a southwest wind. Early in the afternoon we entered Vallevista which according to our map was the nearest post-office to the place where we hoped to make camp. Harvey drew up in front of Hoadley & Son's grocery and went inside to buy gasoline. An old man, whom we took to be Hoadley, senior, rose from his bench on the store veranda and came to the steps to salute his son's customer.

"Can we get out to the shore by this road?" my husband asked, his hand on the car-door as he leaned to look for a guide-post.

"With that proposition behind ye?" Mr. Hoadley eyed our trailer critically. "She leads like a freight-car, eh! But how does she pull in soft ground? The road's a dirt road, through the Italians' truck-gardens."

"Do we *want* to camp in a vegetable garden?" I hastily put in, and was ignored.

"We want to get out about where Cascarone Creek comes into the sea?"

"Laguna Point, you mean? That's where you'll just about *be* if you follow that road. There ain't no other road."

"Can you tell us if camping is allowed on the Rancho Del Refugio?"

"Sure! You could fix that easy. Italians rent the land. They won't bother you none. You'd have to see Tony Kayding about permission; he's in charge out there—runs the pumpin'-plant. But you won't like that place for a camp. The north wind hits that point something fierce. There ain't no bathin'—water's too cold; surf's full of sand."

"We never bathe!" I hastened to assure Mr. Hoadley; but he knew me for a mere wife by this time and he ignored me too.

"How's the fishing up Cascarone Creek?" my spouse continued.

"Well, the steel-heads are runnin' now, but they're awful small. Children ketch 'em right along—they eat good. You wouldn't call it much for sport if you're a fly-fisherman," he added with a touch of sarcasm.

"Any shore-fishing off the rocks?"

"Oh, yes; if the tide's right. Depends on where you go. You can git sea-perch and black bass;—if the surf's too high you won't git any or if the water's muddy. Fish are queer things! them shore fish all go out to sea when it's full moon.... There's Kayding now. *Oh*, Tony! Come on over here."

We could pick out Tony easily, for he was the only man with leisure, it seemed, to hang about the post-office so early for the mail; the stage was not due for a quarter of an hour. He stood on the outskirts of a little crowd of girls and old women, with his back to the wind, cupping his hands to get a light for his cigarette. He did not look up in answer to this hail, took a puff or two, tossed his match into the dust, and crossed over. There was, however, no rudeness that struck one in this deliberation. It seemed more a slow habit of mind or movement. Still, he sprang lightly enough up on the store veranda without going round to the steps, and with that same unhurried air gave us his silent attention.

Charley had got out to speak to him, and they came down the steps together and looked at our road-map, he pointing out the way across the fields we would have to take, or rather the place of it, for it wasn't down on the map. I remarked the slenderness of his dark hands and the whole of his darkness which sun nor seawind could quite account for, and a soft brilliance in his brown-black eye which I should not have called the light of intellect. In all he was a pleasing person, allowing for some disadvantages of dress and a perfectly tame way of talking, in odd contrast to his colorful physique. Latin blood, one guessed by the names on the store-signs everywhere, cooled by a large admixture from the north; his height and the shape of his head were northern.

The talk lasted some time while I made these observations. He stated in answer to questions that the shore was not high above the beach; it rose in benches, low benches running out into reefs or points like the one we aimed for, and there were no trees.

"I should think it might be lonely?" For the first time he looked at me. "Laguna Point is over a mile from the mouth of the creek." ("Just about there," Mr. Hoadley had said.)

"I shall not be lonely," I responded to his look. "People are what we avoid—our fellow campers," I explained amiably. "We want to be the only campers on the beach."

"You will be." He smiled and raised his hat slightly as he met my eyes. "There are shags. They come and sit on the rocks out there."

"What are shags?" I cried, for now he was talking! but my camp-mate dragged him away from me with questions of driftwood and fresh water. These vital details were fully discussed and turned out fairly to my husband's satisfaction. It remained to pay for the gasoline and buy fish-poles of the kind in local use, since a rod and flies were accounted as vanity. Our guide told us he was just now going out to his own place about a mile below our point, and as we were not ready to start yet he would wait for us at the turn and show us our road into the fields.

It was not easy to part from Mr. Hoadley, senior; he wanted to tell us of the days when he had "freighted" on the road we had come and "it was no picnic to cross them grades." He chuckled over his own outfit compared with ours—he had rolled up in a blanket and slept on the ground beside his wagon and carried water to boil his coffee in a five-gallon "kag." He took jealous note of the name advertised on our canvas water-bag seated on the guard forward, tied to a bracket of the car-top. "Git that thing in New York? What's the matter with San Francisco? Can't you git your stuff there?" As we talked, one or two high-powered cars honked by us making in a few hours stations that had been days and nights apart for him and his teams.

"That's all a fairy-story; that ain't real," said he. "There's nothin' to it if you're out for the fun of the road. This here suits me!" He regarded us I think as a gay compromise between his own times and all the luxury of modern wheel-traffic that swept by him day by day, as he mused on his bench and detained travelers in conversation.

We must have kept our attractive guide waiting a rude length of time at the turn. The wind blew and his horse was restless—he could not have heard our apologies, but you would have thought by his manner that his time was ours. He had opened a gate for us which led into a field of stubble, browner stubble than one sees inland in July. "The Italians," as we called henceforth the tillers of these fields, were getting in hay; it dotted the hill in heaps. All one half of the field tipped up against the sky and around the base of it our road went, a narrow track cut through soft black loam. I pointed it out to my gardener, who smiled in silence. Kayding watched us from the gate wade in and wallow through. Looking back to wave our adieus, we saw the marshes that stretch eastward gleaming with tide-water in slits and pools, and the sunlight sleeping on the farther hills. Ahead of us the south wind with its wall of mist seemed to have shortened the day while in the valley it was still afternoon.

Kayding, as if with an afterthought, wheeled his horse and followed us. We waited.

"If you don't like it out there you might try it down my way. You can't miss the place. Take the road down the shore till you come to a big white hotel—"

"Hotel!" I shrieked in the teeth of the wind.

"Closed."

"And you live there, all alone?"

"And the watchman," he replied.

"What does he watch?"

He answered my impertinence very neatly.

"Part of his business is to watch campers." We all laughed. "If you should come down when I'm not there, tell him you have permission to camp wherever you like. My name is Kayding."

Charley gave him our name and when he said "Mrs. Cope," Kayding took his hat clear off and showed a head of thick black curls that needed a barber, his half-boots needed cleaning, and the trousers tucked into them needed a new pair. Nevertheless, if my old cavalry captain could have had him one year or six months, he would have turned him out a faultless trooper. He could ride, of course.

We watched him from our cushions, as the car labored through the field, go swaying up that road with the ocean on one side below it and the valley on the other. He could see what we only felt, as yet, in the wind that came in our faces and rattled our new bamboo fish poles lashed to the guards. On the hill he struck a hard trot and was gone down the other side.

"How do you *feel* when you think we shall never ride again!" I groaned to Charley.

"We have had a good deal of riding," he answered, implying there are other things in life.

But *I* knew how he felt just the same. We dragged our overcoats out of the coat-bag and helped each other on with them and rocked along—very heavy going—through the black, crumbly soil bearing its acres of artichokes and peas and brussels sprouts. We left behind us the gray roofs and cattle-yards where the Italians hide their homes in hollows out of the wind.

Laguna Point, when we reached it, looked as if we might have been its first white discoverers since some straggler of a native race had eaten mussels there and left a heap of bluish shells near a half-burnt log. An old sock trodden into the earth dissolved the illusion. The men went down on the beach and I followed the vestiges of a little path wandering out to the end and stood there in silent outlook on the sea. The place had a singular, lone, concentrated charm—not for a home, of course; there was too little of it.

As the peninsula narrowed there were steep plunges down both sides and it ended apparently in another plunge into the sea, but when I went out carefully with awe of what was coming, there lay the reef below with a path going down, and beyond it was a whole school of rocks in play or in conflict with the surf. Some wallowing in it, some sitting up like old sea-lions letting it wash over their heads and down their slippery faces, others lay flat, a treacherous floor where the tide slid in and swung out again combing the long locks of the kelp plants. Deep water lurked between these and the outer rocks where the shag folk were sitting. Incredibly human they looked, black against bursts of spray and tiny as if dwarfed by distance; as one might make out a shipwrecked company huddled on a barren rock waiting for a sail.

I went over to the other side and watched the men down on the beach; Harvey gathering driftwood, the colonel in his ulster plodding through the sand close under the limestone bluff speering for water. I thought: "He won't stop to change before helping Harvey unpack—he'll make camp in those trousers; he has no others to go back with! Cecily will ask us to dinner; she expects her father to look the same immaculate old soldier. Well; you can't carry everything in a trailer."

While I stood watching our men, another man, very ill-looking, slowly approached and watched us all, standing still a long time. Instantly and primitively I hated the sight of this man. I sniffed him as it were and found him not good. Then I went back along the path and tried to divert my mind; there was a weed grew on the cliff, new to me, with a harsh, sweet, pungent odor—I picked it and smelled it; the stem was sticky and I threw it away.

The man had not moved, but my husband was beside him speaking to him (not snarling!). They were engaged in what looked like an amicable discussion of the place that we called ours. The man pointed to the bluff, here and there. My gracious old colonel not only tolerated his presence, he seemed actually to be consulting him as a stranger might a native, or as one stranger might confer with another. I rushed off on my path again. On the next return it was a huge relief to see Charley's cap appear ascending the trail from the beach. He looked provokingly satisfied.

"Who is that man," said I, "you've been talking to so long?"

"Down there? He's an old Tired Tatters out of a job. He sleeps in the gulch just above us. Eats, I guess, wherever it happens—"

"And do you want him there?"

Charley stared. "He's got water—nothing to dig with but his hands, so it's not much; not enough for us too, though he didn't say that. He says we can get water nearer."

"How long will he be here, do you know?"

"While the weather is good, very likely. He walked down from Sonoma County looking for a job at the cannery at Pigeon Point. Nothing doing, so he's saving board and lodging till better times."

"It's useless to unpack the trailer, then." Charley waited to be sure that he understood me. "If that man stays here, I can't, of course. I should think you'd see that."

"But he isn't here. He's a quarter of a mile away."

"He will be here—down on the beach watching us. I shall think he is, anyhow, whenever my back is turned."

"He isn't watching you; he's filling his water-can. He stares around while it fills. He isn't thinking about you."

"I should be thinking about him."

"But there's nothing wrong about him. I've talked with him. He's a harmless old guy—looks like a ruffian; so would I if I had lived six weeks or six days as he has."

"You know, Charley"—I spoke with the utmost moderation—"I've never roughed it outside of guards. I'm no sport in that sense; you mustn't expect it of me."

"But you said you didn't mind its being lonely?"

"What I mind is its not being lonely enough. You don't want me to share my loneliness with that tramp up the gulch! If I saw him come up that path I should go out to the end, and if he came as far as *that*, I should jump off."

My husband turned and walked away.… Harvey glanced up at us, but getting no signal he sat still on his pile of driftwood and waited. He probably recognized even at that distance a domestic crisis of some kind that had caused a stay of proceedings.

Charley came back again. "Why do you stick in camp all alone? Why not go fishing with us? You needn't fish—take a book. It won't be fishing all the time; we shall want to knock about with the car and see what's here. Doesn't the place suit you?"

I replied it was a perfect gem of a place, the sweetest spot of its size I had ever set foot on.

"Then, great Scott!" My husband could say no more.

"There are a hundred little things I want to do in camp; I expect to live! But I don't want to live with a revolver at my elbow—that's what it would mean."

"But, Lucy—see here now! I know a scoundrel— you don't suppose I'd take risks with you? The man's got the same right here that we have. We're tramps ourselves."

"He may be my brother, but I don't want him so near. And that settles it as far as I'm concerned. We came here to be happy—what fun is it trying all the time to control one's nerves? Why can't we go and look at the other place, where what's-his-name and the watchman live? I like the idea of a watchman."

Charley had been rolling a cigar in his fingers; he lighted it now and figuratively speaking, we put on our coats again and shook hands. I have not married a small man.

"Well, cheero, girl! The water's hard, anyhow. It's a beastly bore in camp, bad water and not enough of it."

He gave Harvey his signal; he rose and shouldered a load of driftwood; in answer to a second signal he dropped it and left it there. And we swung off the point which in fact we had barely swung onto with the trailer, and drove as fast as we could travel down the shore.

My husband reads maps, of course, as a musician reads a sheet of music. He had picked out this spot after long study of the Coast Survey's charts, which go into lovely details, names of all the old ranches and all—he knew about the soil and the crops it bears and about the gray-covered skies and brooding fogs and frequent great days of sunshine. What more he knew I cannot say, but it was the place of his dream, never seen, yet he went straight there and found it just as he had foretold; which is path-finding, and I was vain of it, yet I drove him away with loud cries. He was puzzled and bored and cross, but his patience held out, and when he gave up he did it as if it were naught and the incident was closed. He did indulge in one little wicked taunt:

"That hotel, I expect, will be the worst thing you ever set eyes on; don't faint away when you see it, please! We've got to camp somewhere to-night."

Nothing could have prepared one for the shock of that hotel, on such a spot. The sea took no notice of it, of course, nor the moors nor the sandy tracts for three miles in sight where the tide came rolling in with its loneliness of pause and sound. A tank-tower rose beside it joined to the second-story by a bridge passageway. It wasn't a bad feature and it meant artesian water. Harvey's first chore after the tents were up was to go for some, and Charley went with him to announce ourselves. Kayding was not there, but the watchman treated us handsomely and gave us enough firewood for night and morning.

We lay awake a little while in our respective cots on either side of the tent-pole close to each canvas wall. Through the curtain, tied back, we saw a pale glimmer of moonlight struggling with the incoming fog. Kayding's or the watchman's black cat went past on stealthy feet;—"Woosh! Get out, there!" came from my partner's side, and I knew he wasn't asleep yet.

"Of course," I resumed, thinking of the day's failure on my part, "when you do go back to Nature, the first thing you meet is fear—Fear! I was just natural this afternoon. It's only after we're civilized we become ashamed of fear, except the fear of germs. And then is just the time when some old germ of savagery we've forgotten all about may spring out on us, and all we've taken for granted, for ages, in our brother man, in one moment is lost. And just so with the nations. England has laughed at fear—the most civilized people in the world. But she isn't laughing now!"

We didn't know yet what England would do. She had asked for those assurances about Belgium and Belgium had answered and France, but Germany had not and it seemed a very sinister silence.

"Well, I wouldn't, if I were a nation, or even a woman, cultivate a consciousness based on fear.—There's that damned cat again!"

It would have been as well if Harvey had cultivated a consciousness based on fear of cats, for next morning our ham, which he had suspended from the up-tilted tongue of the trailer, we found had been chewed by something on hind-legs in the nature of a cat, the same, no doubt, that slipped past our tent in the moon-struck fog.

But it was cold next morning! The watchman's wood being large for our tent-stove, the fire started slowly and the colonel, who is a hasty man when chilly after his bath, stuffed in a piece of pitch-pine and when all got going together we were fairly driven out of the tent; but the soft fog curtained us in, and we *did* have such a good breakfast! Harvey cook, indeed! This, of course, was one of the things we took on trust.

Camp-life means concentration, and like other forms of concentrated living it has its little daily slips and deliverances, but it really pays now and then to strip one's self down to "food and fire and candle-light"; it is then, truly, God rests one's soul. In a week, I had written up all my back-correspondence and had forgotten the word "tired!"

II

It was my first day alone in camp and I had
just dated my first camp-letter, seated in front of my
husband's army trunk using it as a secretary. I was
writing to Katherine, the one of our three daughters
who I knew would be most indulgent to her parents'
latest hobby. This is no reflection on the other two.
Cecily had been polite about the trailer, though her
own hobbies were more apt to follow the fashion. She
did not know any people who went about with tent-
poles wagging behind them; it made one rather a show
and it sounded squalid unless you explained in detail,
which is tiresome, that one's elderly parents really
did preserve the decencies and some of the comforts,
even in camp. But she did not, I imagine, boast of our
adventure. Patty, of course, was too far away and too
absorbed in being newly married to care very much,
so long as we weren't ill, what we were up to. Letters

to her were so far behind the date, anyhow, a few days
more or less made no difference in their freshness,
nor did Patty's mother repine at the thought that
her "baby" no longer lived to any great extent in her
mother's letters, nor counted the days till they came.
Patty was a very normal young wife.

So it was to Katherine this letter made its appeal.
The word is not too strong. We had not seen her
since we came home, after three years! She was our
disappointment (because we thought she ought to
have been a boy), and our pride because of how she
had turned out in spite of it, and in some ways our
despair. We were getting to be afraid of her decisions
which we knew could not be influenced beyond a
certain point not measured by affection; we no longer
doubted she was a loving child. But our wonder and
uncertainty about her kept us in suspense. I had not,
as I was writing, the least idea whether, in spite of our
long separation and our own stated plans whereby she
knew it would be difficult for us to go East, I could,
by putting my heart into this plea, induce her to come
out and camp with us and help us, as I cunningly put
it, to choose our home. And then—but that was too
breathless a hope to hazard prematurely, that last plea.

Katherine's way of taking this camping-scheme,
her joining us, in short, would, I felt, be something
of a test—not of her affection: that were a cruel
test—but of the ground we now stood on. For we
had parted with considerable pain on both sides. Was
she still resolved to keep her life apart, distrusting our

comprehension and doubting our sympathy, as perhaps we had given her reason to do?

I had scarcely written a page, seated with my back to the open tent-door, when steps went by and, looking out, there stood Kayding in front of the cook-tent which was inhospitably tied from top to ground. I went out and explained that Charley and Harvey and the trailer had gone for a load of driftwood from the Point, and asked him to stop and pay me a little visit, leading the way as I spoke back to the "house."

"This is the canteen," I said.

"May I leave these in your canteen?" He opened the mouth of a bag nearly full of fresh green peas, just picked and positively dewy. I squealed with delight.

"Peas, real peas! Who ever heard of such a thing in camp?"

He reminded me that they grew by the carload just back of us. Yes, I said, but I had supposed they vanished in those cars to San Francisco wholesale. He made light of his gift somewhat further, but I took the peas themselves quite seriously and begged his indulgence if I shelled a mess of them right then and there, so Harvey might cook them for dinner. It was like gobbling them down before his face and eyes without offering him a share; but a prudent mind foresaw how they would help out conversation too— he was sure to be difficult to talk to. And after he had gone I wished to finish my letter.

We sat in the lee of the tent, I with my pan of peas in my lap and a newspaper on the ground weighted down with stones, for the pods. We spoke of the weather, of course; the south wind was still blowing, which he said was most unusual—for it to last so long.

But didn't he love these gray days? Surf was so beautiful on a gray sea. By noon it would be all sunshine; and those great clouds in the east lounging along the moors. The place was lovely! We were wonderfully suited here, I told him in a gush.

Perhaps he thought it chiefly gush; he answered, almost apologizing. We had not come, he said, at the best season. "We don't have so much fog earlier or later in the summer."

But we did not need their flattering weather, I told him; any old weather they happened to have on hand seemed good enough to us. And I asked if he had always lived there. He was born, he said, on one of those farms back of us.

Ah, then he couldn't know anything about it!

Why did I say that?

"I will say, then, that you can't know till you have gone away and seen other places to compare this with."

I labored it out as to a child, and he answered as simply as a child, "But I don't expect to go away."

There was a pause, and I inquired about his name which had a Scandinavian sound to me somehow.

"My grandparents came from Bergen," he said. "They spelled it Kaeden. I believe my grandfather had some German blood. He was a shipmaster in the Alaskan trade. They lived in Portland. He was lost at sea when my father was a boy, just big enough to hang about the docks. His mother—my grandmother—saw the sailor was in him too and she didn't want it; she was afraid. So she moved down to California and put him in a store in San José."

"That *was* a change," said I. "And then?"

"Well, he grew up there and married my mother. Her name was Hernandez."

"And that is why you have a Spanish look—with your Kaydings of the north? Her people were early Californians?" I used the politer word, but he rejected it.

"They were Mexicans, yes. Old settlers in the Santa Clara Valley. I suppose they had some Spanish blood; the first of them came up with the padres—he was a soldier. He had an Indian wife."

I suggested they could hardly have had any others. "We don't hear of Spanish ladies coming over with the Conquistadores."

"But they were Mexicans," he repeated.

"And owned half the valley, I suppose?"

"More of it than they knew or cared; they had very little money, but they didn't need it. They were too lazy to want anything. Then, after the gold rush, their cattle went up—such prices they never dreamed of. They sold their herds as fast as they could and threw the money away; gambled it away and gave it to any one. They thought there was no end to it. They didn't know how to save anything. When they got in debt they mortgaged their land; thousands of acres for a few hundred dollars; and when they couldn't pay interest, the land went. What a foreclosure was they hardly knew. It looked all fraud to them. This is one side of the story. You hear a great many sides."

In the pause that followed he had been looking about him, glancing at the tent interior behind us through the tied-back curtain, at our stovepipes and our dish-towels flapping on the tent-ropes and Harvey's blue enamel-lined dishpan inverted on the home-made bench he called his sink.

"You are very" — he paused for the word— "luxurious campers."

I remarked he must not say that to my husband. He prided himself on cutting out all "frills": only what was necessary, in the smallest possible compass. "That's his training. He's an old West Pointer," I bragged to that Infant.

He missed at first the "Point," so to speak. I explained. "He's an army man, retired now, of course. This is our first journey since we were married, entirely free from orders or the shadow of orders. That's why we are such children about it, and why he's such an old hand."

My listener seemed to reflect a moment. "There must be great education for a man in army life."

I said there was great curtailment of his wishes and his own "way." But that was discipline.

"Perhaps it's discipline I mean," said Kayding. "It's something most of us don't seem to have, unless we are so poor that we don't have anything else."

It struck me he must have had an idea or two under that crop of cowboy curls. "And now," he continued, "that your husband can do as he likes—"

I finished his sentence for him:—"What will he do with his freedom? That *would* be a question, if any one could ever say he was free. We shall decide first what things we can't do and turn our eyes away from them. We know, for instance, that 'we' have no head for business; my husband could not sell anything. And we'd lose what little we have if we went in for schemes; and he couldn't compete with younger men on salaries; and he doesn't want to live in Washington and sit around in clubs. So—" I paused; the vacuum of my listener's deep attention (not the vacuum of his mind, for I perceived he had a mind) drew my words from me in a stream—there was always a head on sufficient for that stream; but feeling safe with him somehow, so out of our lives in every way, I rambled on: "And so we shall live in the country and save on clothes— my clothes—and keep down our flesh—his, you may have noticed! He intends to spend his days in the two pursuits he calls God's best gifts to man: fishing and gardening."

"Fishing and gardening," my good-child listener repeated unconsciously. "That is what they are all doing down here; but they are not men of any education hardly."

"So much the duller for them."

"That's true, of course," said Kayding. "You don't mean gardening for market?"

"Well, hardly till we have learned how. But be sure we shall garden for all there is in it."

"And it might be here?"

"Why, of course, it might be here!—and all this beauty thrown in. We picked out this shore on the deck of a transport three thousand miles away in mid-ocean. My husband is a map-fiend and we are both map-dreamers; we've always been discovering dwelling-places we couldn't dwell in. But now we think, if our daughters don't order us out of this place, we shall dig ourselves in right here."

"But there are no people at all of the kind—of your kind?"

"Ah, but we have to be more than one kind. Army people learn to be good mixers. We've lived in places lonelier than this, yet with neighbors—sometimes in the same house—whom we couldn't choose nor get away from. That was discipline! This is rest. Here we could see as little of our neighbors, or as much, as we like, granting we behave ourselves; and for guests, no one would ever come who didn't love this sort of thing or love us. You see how good it would be?"

I had not been talking all this time to him; I was thinking aloud to Katherine, in the words of the letter not written yet. He answered musingly:

"I never heard of anything so natural that sounded somehow so strange."

"Perhaps we've forgotten what is natural," said I. "We make such an artificial thing of happiness...." The peas weren't finished quite; I had heaped my pan

knowing how the men would make them disappear.
Kayding leaned and took a pod and shelled it and
let the peas drop through his fingers (and again I
noticed the shape of his hand). "But isn't all grown-up
happiness 'artificial'? Human happiness—animals are
not happy or unhappy unless they are in pain. But we
can be happy by thinking we are, or not thinking."
Had the Infant ever known sorrow, I wondered.
He seemed to have no visitors, no one belonging to
him.... I rose to carry my peas to the cook-tent and he
followed with the pods bundled in newspaper.

"*Not* over the cliff!" I screamed, as he was about
to throw—"We'll bury them after dinner. You don't
suppose we insult this place with our garbage!"

"You are the first campers here who didn't!"

"We love it already."

"I love it. When you spoke about the shore just
now I felt as if you were talking of my father and my
mother."

We stood on the edge of the cliff looking down. I
said that I didn't understand so much surf with so little
wind; we had had it for days!

"It's the ground-swell," said he. "Something has
happened out at sea."

"What is out there? China? If it were the Atlantic,
we might talk of ground-swells.... Oh, hark!"

Down the shore there was a rock with a cavern
in it or a hole; wave after wave rolled up to the mouth
and broke and went seething in. But every five minutes
or so (just then we heard it) a great slow comber came

towering on, gained the entrance at full height and crashed into that hollow place with an immeasurable sound, the note of a gun deepened to a thousand guns, but infinitely far away, dying down "the shingles of the world." I raised my shoulders in a shiver.

"Yes, that's the old ground-swell," said Kayding. "There's trouble out there somewhere. It means a big storm—"

"It means the war!"

He looked at me vaguely. "The war in Europe? But that's on the other side."

I agreed it would take longer for that ground-swell to reach our side. We smiled at each other, I not to seem superior in my apprehensions of one sort or another, he in simple courtesy. He was a child, but a gentle, wistful child with a delicate mind slowly gathering impressions that would become a very exceptional consciousness, I prophesied. I decided that even such a garrulous old person as myself would have blushed for all that babbling, if there hadn't been this atmosphere of refinement and peaceful understanding about him.

I watched him go up the path to the hotel; such an unaggressive personality to be lodged in that towering landmark of ugliness! To occupy it alone! The watchman had his own little cottage snug down near the garage.

III

Still thinking of Kayding, I returned to my letter and rattled off something about him which on re-reading wouldn't do; it sounded like a slur. He was not easy to describe with anything like adequacy, and why describe him at all, to Katherine? My letter I have called a plea, but of course one couldn't go on that tack with her; one had to be prepared for her humor. Dithyrambs about the place—that wouldn't do either. In short, my pen in writing this letter traveled a narrow path, and I was but feebly interested, when the men came home, with their haul of driftwood which looked as if it might last all winter. There was a message Kayding had left for my fisherman which I had transferred to paper "lest we forget." I handed him the paper:

"Chinaman's Rock for pompanos, but not till after this surf goes down."

And then I went out upon my usual beat, old
wheel-tracks worn in the coarse grass and sand that
already I had made into a path along the first bench
above us. Eastward rose the moors, dark, wind-slanted
grass against the sky, reminding one of Jane Eyre's
drawing and Rochester's question, "Who taught you to
draw wind?"

Night was coming on in thickening gray, not a
gleam of sunset; but punctual to the hour when the
bugles used to sound retreat, Pigeon Point Light flared
out, a big red star. Almost every evening, while smoke
poured out of the cook-tent stovepipe, I walked my
path outside and watched that light arise and go out;
you count ten between the flares and if the rays are
spread on fog, as they were that night, they stream
out seaward like a searchlight. I walked fast and saw
nothing in particular; my thoughts were pressing
company. A mother's thoughts at my age are so often
a review of her own mistakes with her children. I had
been saying to myself some words of the nurse I had
with me in Arizona when my little son was born—we
laughed at them then, but they were long remembered.

"He's a fine boy, m'm, but don't ye set your heart
on raisin' him. We mostly learns on the first one."

Not everything! With Cecily I seemed to have
made all the mistakes there was not time to make
before. From girlish ignorance and over-confidence
I rushed to the opposite extreme, haunted by the
warnings of experience and dogged by doctors' rules.
For two wretched years I forsook my husband on the

frontier that this child should have all the safeguards before and after birth that our first one had lacked. Those years deepened the hold fear had gained on my half-educated mind. And so as a growing child Cecily was too much hovered over and prevented. As a girl she was lazy and lumpy and unattractive; and then, in one school year in the East, she budded deliciously, and came out to us and unfolded before her mother's enraptured eyes. She was so—delicious is the word— in her coloring, her bewitching eyes, her appealing softness and indefiniteness of expression, that one did not observe or did not mind her triviality. What wonder if she thought about clothes when they were so madly becoming; and about the lads when the lads were all thinking about her!

But there were no lads! Cecily's school-days ended just in time for her to share our exile to a little two-company post in the far Northwest, in a country of old Indian wars. Its garrison had once safeguarded the few white settlements where Indian wars usually begin, and the prosperous town that had grown out of those settlements near the post was even duller from a girl's point of view than the post itself. Its officers were just-married lieutenants, a stout major who drank, acting-quartermasters, and so on, and the invaluable medical officer absorbed in his microscope. For three years we were at Fort Donelly—three years wasted for that enrapturing child.

Since this was my secret thought, it seems evident that in falling in love with my first grown-up daughter

I had revived some of the vanities as well as excitements
of the original experience. Cecily's sudden flowering
undoubtedly went to her mother's head. I longed
to show this surprising creature to the old friends
at home who had known her only as an awkward,
infelicitous school-girl. I thought of dances I would
dress her for, I thought of marriage, of course, and
no ordinary marriage for Cecily. What I meant by an
ordinary marriage was probably such as I had made,
taking better and worse fortune as it came, life and
death, of course, but drudgery also, risks and cramped
quarters, and climates that were a strain, and journeys
and packing and all manner of hustling and grime. I
had seemed to work up to it somehow; at times had
even got a sense of triumph and high achievement out
of it. But I couldn't see Cecily living my life. It was for
her sake I longed for the big posts where she would
meet other than men in uniform. And of them all
the Presidio was the blue ribbon post, the goal of my
desires.

Meanwhile Katherine, who should have been a
boy, lived exactly like one and learned whatever her
father's son if he'd had one would have had to learn.
The most daring little rough rider on her stubborn
cayuse, the best shot with her thirty-two; she copied all
the soldiers' stunts on the bars and at the hurdles; she
could make her father lose his breath in their fencing-
bouts. And her rapid little brain chimed with all the
rest like a set of bells. She "loved it" at Fort Donelly.
My mother died the year it was Katherine's turn to go

East to school; there was no grandmother's house for her at vacations. She came home, and felt that the West was home, in a sense unknown to Cecily.

At last the order came to pack and go; the coveted post was ours. One may have cause to fear the sudden granting of one's ignorant, impatient prayers. If I had looked into that comer of my heart where worldliness had taken a decided start, I might have blushed to detect the wish for a rich son-in-law. And within two years we had that gift thrust into our faces and we were afraid, but the better fear came too late. It was such thoughts as these, thrown on the solitude of our sea-camp, that kept me awake hours in the night, and that drove me fast along my shore-path. They seemed to point to something tragic looming for Cecily, but I wasn't sure that the real tragedy might not be that Cecily did not seem to mind what would have been tragedy—say for Katherine.

That winter in San Francisco (the second winter) we spent so much money that when it came to reckoning journey expenses, I saw that I should have to give up going East in June to see Katherine in her Commencement robes deliver the Valedictory at St. Helen's. She had done in two years what Cecily barely crawled through in three. It was a much keener disappointment to Katherine than we had imagined. But there was no help for it; she crossed the continent alone. At Green River, where the Oregon Short Line takes off into the Bear Valley country, she got out and breathed the sage-scented air and looked at the strange

red rocks that had been the gateway of home. Speaking
as a girl of eighteen, she never expected to be as happy
again as she had been at Fort Donelly; but this was
because she dreaded San Francisco. It had not escaped
our young Daniel, that new note of worldliness which
had crept into her mother's letters once so full of good
talk between them, but now since Cecily's triumphant
entrance into "society," taken up with a mass of little
things of no interest to a senior at St. Helen's, or brief
and hurried; and this, too, she laid to the change in our
home surroundings. By chance, this prevision of dislike
gained force through the conduct of three conspicuous
young San Franciscans whom she had noticed on the
train.

The news of a great family event awaited her. We
had kept it back because words are better than writing,
and we wanted her with us when the trial came. I knew
that Katherine would take it hard, Cecily's engagement,
out of a clear sky, to a man she had never heard of.
My own consciousness was not free from a sense of
betrayal, of false values, to say the least: but for my
"showing off" of Cecily she never would have met the
young man, and her parents both felt that her beauty
had been the chief attraction for him. Katherine had
made no friend at school to compare in dearness with
this idealized elder sister of whom she never could
see enough. She had been all along a little jealous of
Cecily's new acquaintances in the strange city that had
seemed to go to all our heads. And now to lose her just
as their real companionship was going to begin! She

had yet to see the man—he might prove the reconciling factor.

And then she did see him, the first night at dinner, and he was the youth whose measure she had taken on the train! What if she had known that he was engaged to Cecily! He, of course, that gay boy, Peter Dalbert, had not seen, to notice her, the quiet scorner of his play. Business, as he called it, had taken him East at the lucky date of the Yale-Harvard boat-race. He had been having a royal time and was still "lit up" with its effects as he turned his face westward to his new-made fiancée. He was a young gentleman whose behavior did not always bear out that definition of a gentleman which says he is one who conducts himself the same whether he is conscious of observation or thinks himself alone. Nobody Peter knew was on the train. Two alluring young women who shared the drawing-room took him in tow; it was a merry journey, and one, so far as he knew, without consequences. I am telling what I know now, but did not know then; and I was not, of course, with my girls when they talked him over first alone.

"You don't like him?" Cecily challenged her sister's silence.

"I don't like him as well as I do you. You didn't expect it, did you?"

"You can't bear him! You might as well own it—he asked me what was the matter with you—if you were always like that?"

"I don't suppose it has occurred to him that he's robbing this family. I wanted you myself. It comes too soon—" Katherine began then and there to practice that duplicity we were to be forced to keep up for years, for years!

I fancied I heard slight sounds in Katherine's room that night long after she should have been in bed. I stole to her door; there was no answer to my soft knock.

"Katherine? Are you awake, dear?" I opened the door on a crack. She was in her dinner frock still, a silk robe drawn around her shoulders; she got up from her chair by the fireless grate and snapped on the lights. We looked at each other in dismay.

"What is it?"

"Nothing, mother." Her eyes dropped—"I don't feel sleepy; coffee, perhaps—I'm not used to it at night."

"Don't put me off. What was the matter with you at dinner?"

"Mother, dear, I'm tired; and I've got to make up my mind to a thing I hadn't expected—not for years, at least. You didn't like it at first, did you?"

"Is it the man?"

"Why—I shouldn't want to marry him. But no one I've ever seen would be good enough for Cecy."

I took hold of the robe and drew it close about her; she was pale and shivering. "Will you go to bed now if I go away and don't question you? Do let me make a fire."

"I had a fire; it seems to have gone out."

"It's burned out! You have been sitting here hours. Have you nothing to tell me?"

"Nothing I could really explain; a thing can't be much if you don't know how to put it into words."

"Oh, yes, it can!"

Days later, when Katherine had been driven to own that she did dislike the man, I said, "We must give him his chance. He has a great many friends; some of them I'm sure you would like."

She met his mother next day and she liked her. At least she said she was a clever, commanding sort of person, not in the least common—the implication was plain. Mrs. Dalbert barely tolerated the engagement (this we were quite aware of), but, as we afterwards knew, old friends of Peter's father—she was a widow of large means and influential connections—advised her that Peter ought to marry as soon as possible if he could find a well-bred girl of good principles not afraid to take him. And it might be as well that her family should be strangers, the less likely to have heard tales of his fatuous past. But now that she saw Katherine, she was less content than ever. She must have doubted that Cecily's influence could last; but this girl, if he could have won her, might have made him do anything.

"She's the clever one," she said to me once, and she said it bitterly. She was a great believer in heredity, which, of course, includes marriage; she did not face the fact that she had failed with Peter. He seemed to her still a boy, and he was such a living proof, besides, of her own theories; all his father's past lay behind him, poor fated child. I suppose she had never seen the girl she would not have sacrificed to save her only son. What are good girls for?

Very soon after Katherine's return the engagement was formally announced and the usual gayeties followed. What our young stoic thought as she took her part in them and during all the preparations for the wedding, which was as fashionable as we could afford, no one had leisure to imagine, unless it were her father. Cecily was in a state of almost too obvious elation. She seemed not to miss the little talks and bedtime confidences that would have been natural between sisters under the circumstances. *I* missed them. Katherine kept to herself a good deal and wrote letters to her schoolmates, in particular to a friend, one of the teachers, whom she seemed to care for too seriously to talk much about.

We were left to ourselves during the first days after the wedding; even our neighbors at the Presidio did not call. One evening when his two "girls" were keeping him (the major, since his last promotion) company while he smoked his after-dinner cigar, Katherine suddenly asked him if he thought he could afford to give her the course at Bryn Mawr.

"What, more schools!" More separations, he meant—she misunderstood him.

"Would it cost more than coming out next winter? I'll try and see that it doesn't go on costing so much— and you wouldn't have the trouble of marrying me." The bitter little jest went unanswered in a pause of consternation.

"What does this mean, puss?" her father asked.

"I don't know, daddy. I seem to have got hold of things out here by the wrong handle somehow."

"Can't you take a fresh hold?"

"Why, I'm afraid not, if you want me to do what Cecily did last winter."

"But we don't necessarily," I put in.

"If I stay home—here, it will come to the same thing. I should have to be at Cecy's house a good deal. And I don't care so very much for her new friends, to tell the truth. My fault; but one doesn't enjoy being 'haired up' most of the time—about nothing."

"You put too much emphasis on all that side of her life," said I. "Things will quiet down after a while. Just now she wants to please everybody Peter knows. When it comes to friends, there's a good deal of room for choice—even 'here' as you call it. Give her time."

I regretted "as you call it" as soon as the words were spoken. Katherine answered coldly: "There is her choice of a husband. We can't get away from that."

"Katherine, dear!" I gasped; "we mustn't be disloyal, even by ourselves."

"I don't know how far you expect to carry that, mother. Do you think we'll gain anything by deceiving ourselves?"

"Are you going to be the strong-minded one of the family?" her father quizzed her sternly. He was very much disturbed.

"It doesn't take much mind to see what Peter Dalbert is—" She let herself go. "You don't seem, *any* of you, to have seen what Cecily was doing. How could you, how could you—give her to him!"

She had been speaking from across the hearth keeping us at arm's length, with hurt, proud eyes; now she rushed to her father's lap, hugged him, and hid her face on his shoulder. An ash dropped off the end of his cigar and bit into the folds of her gauzy skirt.

"Take care of her *dress! Do* see what you are doing!" I sprang to crush out the spark before the whole stuff went up in flames about her head.

She sat up and looked at me haughtily:

"You would have to think about my clothes, mother, if I were dying, wouldn't you!"

It was a wounding speech, but mothers understand. Of course, it was forgiven instantly; but her father, all shaken as he was, shouted in his big field voice that hurts like a blow: "Don't *speak* to your mother so! What do you *mean* by it?"

We dropped the subject, having bruised each other enough for that evening, but the question itself could be settled only in one way. American parents give in, as we did. But it broke our simple dream of a home with daughters around us. Long before Katherine would have finished at Bryn Mawr we might be ordered across the world; we were in line for the Philippines. And so it turned out. She was not with us when we made that wonderful voyage two years later; half its meaning was gone, the other half was pure pain. It was a break in the family that to our view lacked the natural sequence of marriage. When we parted with Patty, it was in the old, inevitable way, and to our simple minds her education would be going on through the immemorial problems of marriage and motherhood. But Katherine had joined herself to books and to women of advanced ideas, and we feared these commitments would end in a complete revolt against the old order, a sort of secular taking the veil.

So here we are, I meditated; three daughters and not one we can call our own so far as ever seeing her goes. Katherine, by the way, was the only one (and this was another surprise) who could and did, week by week, not only faithfully but joyously and as if with no effort, make up for absence by her letters. The fullness and richness of this intercourse had come to mean a closer intimacy than had ever marked our home life together; I might have said I had lost her only to find her. But underneath the personal understanding that grew as our love grew, lay those differences which we called the point of view of our two generations. These were waiting.

Katherine, in her share of our correspondence, practiced a holy reticence which ruled out petty criticism of those we knew and loved; also complaints, however wittily set forth. She had not learned this by example—I love a grievance!—nor was it part of her home training as it might have been had that been religious: "Teach me to feel another's woe and hide the fault I see" was not current speech with her nor song. I set it down to sheer manliness and sportsmanlike behavior, the result of college and field life, her way of treating as if they were her own the weaknesses of those who were at her mercy. I revered her example, though it was away above my head. But even I did not ask her questions about Cecily. It would have been of little use—Katherine would never have put confidences in writing if she had had any to impart. Counting the weeks and months and often a year between the sisters' visits, I knew she must be as much of a stranger to Cecily's real life as I was.

I was thinking of Cecily now, so near us, yet I knew she would find some excuse week by week for not coming down. It was only natural, nor did we want her very much. Tent-hospitality is extremely selective. Servants don't mix well at all, not the kind by whom Cecily was surrounded. Two of a trade as they were, there was no common ground between Harvey and the proud person who drove Cecily's cars, and five minutes of our black adobe soil would finish the shoes of her uniformed nurse, if she brought the little boys—but of course she wouldn't, though they would adore it!

I smiled over our own times past when old Shannon, our striker, had been whiles nursemaid to our little army girls, and none could have been more lively and faithful on the job. How he used to take them down at stable-call to watch the troopers in their white jackets grooming the rows of handsome horses; it was a bay troop and a horse was "condemned" for too many hairs in his tail, as it were.

Well, if Cecily should come we should have to
pray for a day when we could "eat" outside; no verb less
primitive could fit our customs in the matter. It was
doubtful if she could stand them, seated knee to knee
almost, and elbows touching, at our restricted table,
unless she had the whole sea and sky as a background.
The first lesson of camp-life (I don't say I had learned
it) is to keep one's mind off trifles or one loses "the
savor of rest." Cecily's life functioned so elaborately
and on such standards of perfection in material ways
that we were frankly afraid of her eye upon us, and no
doubt we were narrow in this, too.

We were seated that evening after dinner on two
camp-chairs side by side, like Abraham and Sarah, in
the door of our tent. A fire in the tent-stove warmed
our knees; Abraham in high boots; several inches
of Sarah's ankles showing in gray Scotch stockings.
We breathed the sweet, strong air and looked at the
darkling shore. The surf was as soothing as the silence it
broke, or which I broke, as I frequently did.

"Well, it's lucky that hotel 'stays put' and we know
where it is, and that we haven't got eyes in the back of
our heads," I said, or repeated, for I had said it before.
"How did they ever come to build it here—such a
useless and profitless monstrosity?"

"It wasn't supposed to be profitless. The Ocean
Shore Road was to have come in here; that's part of it
you walk on every day, and this is the borrow-pit—not

that it is a pit. But that's why no grass grows on it and we pave our tents with beach-pebbles."

"Beach-grass would be sweeter."

"Pebbles last, and when we want to brighten them up and keep down dust, we've only to spill a little water on the bedroom floor."

"Yes," I laughed; "and, anyhow, our tule mats last longer in this damp air."

"And we last longer!"

"Go on and tell about the railroad. Why didn't it go through?"

"You'll have to ask some of the San Franciscans who lost money by it. I suppose in time it will go through."

"Then if we do settle on anything here, hadn't we better buy before that time? A railroad coming in would send things kiting, wouldn't it?"

"If a railroad came along this shore, all the old fields back of it would be cut up into parcels of land, with a station just above us. Can't you imagine it here on Sundays?"

"Then we could sell our parcel at a large advance and go somewhere else." This was only by way of argument.

"We're too old for that," Charley answered seriously. "We don't want to be chased around by railroads."

"We want all we *do* want, of civilization, without having to give up this! Think of our sitting here with nothing human in sight—if we don't look at the hotel—and having our mail every day and fresh eggs and butter and a washer-woman and San Francisco only six hours away! Whatever the railroad might do to us couldn't be worse than that hotel."

"Unless it were open—crammed with the sort of people who would like it."

"I've written to Katherine, anyhow. I expect to write to all the girls."

"Aren't you in a hurry, rather? It's a big shore; we haven't begun to see it yet."

"It will be two months before we can hear from Patty."

"I don't think our plans will interest Patty much for some little time to come."

"I want to hear from them all. The money we put into a home is really theirs."

"If you insist on looking at it that way," my husband smiled.

"But it *is* that way. We don't want to sink all we've got into something that will never do them any good. Nor their children."

"Which child do you expect to lure out here to live with us on this shore?"

"You know which! I could pray for the words that would bring her."

"You know that words won't do it, nor the place— if Katherine has her mind made up. But we might have a good summer out here. You'll fetch her if you don't ask too much."

"I ask! I'm as secret as the grave."

Charley laughed. "You can make yourself felt if you try."

"No; I want to be convincing. Feeling is not enough with Katherine. If she thinks it would be a waste of life out here doing nothing, as she would call it, she'll renounce us and life too. If she hasn't already," I sighed.

"That's it exactly. We can't annex them, and we can't fit our plans to theirs when we don't know what they are, nor they themselves, perhaps. So we might as well do as we like. They won't remember us when we're gone by what we leave them."

It was quite true: we hadn't seen so very much of the shore—I hadn't. I'm not fond of motoring unless there are miles to be swallowed in a certain number of hours, or a great panorama of country unfolding as you fly—just tooling around to see what's to be seen within walking distance doesn't appeal to me. I prefer to walk. I hadn't walked—hiked—for the simple reason that I was so content in that one spot with morning and evening and the tides and change of skies making each day different from the day before.

My man woke up next morning with a pain in his shoulder that caused him to grunt as he made the fire. I asked if he were going fishing with that shoulder.

"'Co'se, honey; how else we gwine to live!" When he's happy he drops into Uncle Remus talk; when he is very happy he becomes nautical. In his far-off boyhood he had played with boats. We talked loud in the tent because the tide was high, thundering at the foot of our cliff stairway and all up seething white over the rocks. As he hauled on his "short pants" one of the side-pockets heavy with coin of the realm (pounds of which he insists on carrying around with him) flopped outside of the waist-band.

"Hi! Pocket over the rail!" he shouted, whereby I knew there were adventures in the wind. At breakfast he asked, "Like to go fishing with us this morning for a change?"

"Where?" I inquired.

"Out on a little point you've never seen."

"Any particular point? I mean any particular point to my seeing it?"

"Never can tell. You'd better come along."

From him, this was enough to start the wildest conjectures…. We drove some three miles down the coast road and crossed the trestle over Bean (Frijole) Creek. Halfway up the next hill we turned in by a fence, left the car, and crawled under the wires and tramped across a sea-pasture—horses grazing at a distance—plenty of distance; and we set foot on that Point called by the name of the ranch, Del Refugio. It is really two points thrust out like a thumb and forefinger from a peninsula shaped like a broad hand. On the summit the thumb is very high, the highest land around. You felt like "stout Cortez," as I remarked to my husband he looked ('specially the stoutness) when you got up there, in the face of the whole Pacific. This peak makes a lee against the north wind

for a little sunny plat big enough for a house and wee
garden—but garden! all over the place, the whole of it
that wasn't rock, and crusting the rocks themselves and
clambering down the face of them—all those stunning
sea-growths that show the fatness of the soil. I sat on
this beautiful stuff as on cushions, I went crushing
through it knee-deep with the smell of it like Lebanon
on my garments (tell it not that it was probably tar-
weed!). The rocks were splendid creatures—all sorts,
like a drove of strange monsters tethered at the base of
the cliff, sea-grazing as it were; and the surf rolled in
on beaches south and north, the south beach flinging
a white arm around the little bay which Bean Creek
tries to get into across a sand-bar that backs water half
a mile up the ravine. All sorts of things we said might
occur up that ravine; flowers and fishing and even still-
water bathing at high tide.

We drove home, very silent, and we sat and
dreamed by our tent-fire. It was scarcely worth while
to exchange words in our mutual content. We were
even mean enough to be glad no one could camp on
that Point without the labor of fetching water from
Bean Creek. If we ever should own it, to build would
mean sinking a well to begin with. I was not afraid.
My husband could do foolish things with money, but
he had a long-distance wisdom at times that money
cannot buy. He has vision. Still, it would be safer,
as I wrote to Katherine astutely, for her to come out
and look after us and see that we didn't make geese of

ourselves. The place laughs at prudence, I told her; it says as plain as words: "It is only heaven that is given away." This was a second letter, written after we had seen the Point.

IV

Cecily's answer came first. It was affectionate and slightly condescending. We were "you dears," and she reminded us that we were not young enough to be romantic unless we could be comfortable, a fact we had taken some account of ourselves. "You'll never be able to keep a decent servant in that place all winter, and if you left it you would need a caretaker always on the spot. You wouldn't be near enough to make any use of me, and when I go to stay anywhere I need the mountains. What you want is a little bungalow in the foothills for the months when it isn't pleasant here. Then a cozy flat where we could see something of you; and you could lock it up and go East or abroad or anywhere you fancied at short notice. I spoke to Madam Dalbert about the land. She thinks it will rise in value very slowly. It's not popular, that shore—or it's too popular. People who build handsome homes go to places where their friends are, like Tahoe or the Monterey coast. I should be afraid it would turn out a sort of Dago settlement, if the railroad did go through."

"Well, what does Cecy say?" her father asked tolerantly. He probably guessed what she would say if she spoke her mind.

"She thinks we shall want to rip up and go traveling every little while. She can't imagine a winter down here.… Read it yourself; she is really anxious about us old folk. She wants us to be safe—as if we ever had been!"

It had been a form, however, consulting Cecily. Any use we might make of our money would not affect her or her children appreciably.

Katherine's answer came promptly in a telegram: "Start for San Francisco Aug. 1. Wire you from Cecily's." So *that* was perfect—no more thus far could be asked of her. Charley went up to town and bought a third tent and furniture, and I began to hector Harvey a little on matters not hitherto considered in my bailiwick. I infringed as to dish-towels, suggesting they might be boiled perhaps oftener than once a week; also that a little of the sea-darkness would come off our solid tin silverware with a touch of polish now and then. But here the chef interfered: Harvey was doing well enough for us; to set up a new and hypercritical standard suddenly in the name of Katherine was unfair to both. If Katherine wasn't satisfied, she could boil the dish-towels herself, or go back to Cecily where she would never see a dish-towel. Only he found words more humorous, not being a bitter person.

Harvey drove to town early on the day before the day, to fetch the new camp-stuff ordered from San Francisco. There was very little of it, and it all folded up or collapsed or made less of itself in some way. My happy Old Man went about tightening tent-ropes and driving in pegs, setting up the profiles of our tents to suit the eye of a West Pointer. I saw him next mounted on a pile of boxes attaching a guy-rope to the forward tent-pole of our tent. The south wind still prevailed contrary to expectations, and the tent, which faced that way, puffed its cheeks out with the sun shining through it like a paper-lantern. As it was blue-green in color, of a thin, tough material soaked in paraffin, the comparison is quite unforced. I had written hurriedly to Cecily to send me a hat proper for a woman of my age to wear in camp. The hat had just come—I needed a friend!—but my husband was too busy to sympathize.

Kayding had been told of our great event. In his life of infinitesimal happenings no doubt it had caused a quickening of curiosity which he relieved, I think, by watching from his height whenever he had leisure (and he had a good deal) our feverish activities in the camp below. He strolled down for a few minutes that evening, and I, being as full of my day's work as little Mrs. Tittlemouse, started to show off its results, but checked myself in fear of my husband's sarcasm. On his way up the path, though, I saw him stop in front of the new closed tent, its virgin canvas white in the moonlight; then he looked up at the moon herself. My eyes followed his, and it was startling to behold her sailing through a clear space she had made for her beauteous self amidst swirls of fog.

Next morning before we drove away to meet Katherine, I with my own hands laid down the new grass mats on the floor of fresh pebbles bright from the last tide, tenderly, not to disturb their leveled smoothness. This was Harvey's offering, all unasked, of course; sacks of them he had carried on his back up from the beach by the steep cliff-path. It was a dear little cell, a mermaiden's bower, if you could have caught one and landed her and wanted to make her feel at home. There were no tree-shadows on its snow-white walls; and the sound of miles of surf came booming through and it smelled inside of sea-breezes and driftweed.

Our rendezvous was in front of a little roadhouse at Half-Moon Bay. I can smile now as I think of that meeting. It was a family comedy, and its contrasts would have amused an appreciative observer. The daughters were there awaiting us, seated in Cecily's new sedan which she drove herself. They both looked charming to us, but they would hardly have been taken for sisters nor for the daughters of such an old pair as we appeared that morning after our early camp-breakfast and drive through the fog. Cecily was dressed for city driving in such a little jewel-box as the new

sedan, Katherine for hopping out of it and dashing
through a small crowd of Half-Mooners gathered to the
show, to embrace her father in the middle of the street;
he in high-boots, oiled, fish-pants, and reefer buttoned
to the chin (pants had been mended in the seat, the
consequence of hours on his favorite fishing rocks).
Our car had not seen the inside of a garage in two
weeks, prowling up and down the soft roads meanwhile
and across fields and leaky ditches: smeary wind-shield,
dark brass, dry mud on the guards and caking the
tires, and the top as gray as a tramp's old derby. Cecy's
smile tightened a little as she looked at us; she must
have been thankful her chauffeur wasn't with her. But
Katherine was in her father's arms returning his big hug
and waving one free hand at me. She was unaltered,
only thinner, more confident and gay in manner,
though she might have been just then a little excited.
The same intense smile, the sallow rose complexion,
daring dark-blue eyes and eyebrows straight as a
dart; the look between eyes and mouth, of spirit and
power and sweetness. Oh, sweetness! I cannot describe
Katherine; I don't believe any one could who had ever
felt her: her strange little face, that no portrait has
preserved, so unregular, unpretty, but so fascinating.

I watched her straighten back from her father's
arms and take in with smiles his new circumference,
that great circle which a swordbelt confines; and he
told me with glee that she whispered, "Once around a
general, *four times* around a lieutenant!" Then she left
him, to argue with Cecily the question of her driving

back with us a little way and sharing our picnic lunch (but Cecy had engagements to prevent), and got into our car beside me.

We held each other's gaze at first, shrinking, but more secure with every second; there could be no real change, and nothing had been lost.

"Little gypsy mother—so brown!" Katherine murmured, chuckling softly. "And what a jolly hat!"

"Don't speak of it! I wrote to Cecy to send me a hat—she did, for a girl of sixteen!"

"Well, I know a lady of a certain age who can wear it!" We talked artificially at first, but we had the real thing there, as safe as human intercourse can be at such a pitch of feeling with beliefs and counter-beliefs underneath. Still, as long as there is a mind— Katherine's mind, let me add; I can reason a little at times, but not under high pressure. However, one mind is enough where love is.

I wondered what our two girls had talked about on their drive down the long coast road, that morning. Cecy very possibly had taken that opportunity (for Cecy is practical) to enlist Katherine's influence, who was known to be able to do anything with her father, against the rash purchase which so tempted their youthful parents. To build a house on a barren rock, without water, without a tree, where no self-respecting servant would consent to stay! I was sure our city-girl— not born a city-girl—would have tried to persuade Katherine of her duty in the case, taking her silence for sympathy. Katherine, of course, would have been silent; she hated arguments.

"I must get out and speak to Cecy," said I, with the old idea that the driver of a vehicle must stick to the box.

"Let her get out!"

She had done so, and came across to us at the moment escorted by her father bearing a sumptuous basket of fruit, the pick of the market, which she had brought us. We all met with smiles, and parted with smiles and kisses and the beach-car and the city-car went their opposite ways.

"Remember!" were Cecily's last words to her sister; "and come to me soon for a nice long visit."

Katherine leaned back with one quick big sigh, when we were fairly started down the coast and the great view of the bay burst upon us. (So far as we have seen the world, I know of nothing like it.) "Let's go on, folks, and have lunch in camp. I want to get home!" Her father looked back at her; their eyes met in silence. He sat smoking one cigar after another as fast as the wind burned them out. Occasionally he threw in a word about the view or answered a question of Katherine's.

"Think you can stand it without trees? You won't see a tree while you're with us."

"I'm glutted with trees and houses and people. Who wants trees! It's the plains—where they cut down to the river; it's the Snake River plains, only the river is *that!*"

Off seaward the fog-bank brooded and the horizon was lost. We all gazed in silence, and I saw what she meant.

"But such a different sky!" I said.

"It's a mothering sort of sky. No wonder everything grows here. You're a pair of wise old birds, and I knew it. Cecy can go to grass!"—Proof of my conjecture, and that Katherine had been faithless to the trust.

We drove fast and reached camp lunchless and hungry about two o'clock. The camp had been visited; some one had tied to the outside of my tent-curtain a bunch of heliotrope fresh-picked and loaded with perfume. Kayding alone could have done it, and I knew he had meant it for Katherine in token of her coming to the shore. Her father knew this, too, and it seemed to vex him.

"Who does this sort of thing?" Katherine looked at me quizzically. "Who's she enslaved now?"

"It's that 'wild gazelle' on the hill she's taming. He eats out of her hand!"

"We eat out of *his* hand and drink out of his cup; see it up there?" I pointed to the tank-tower. "We get all our water from him and he simply gorges us on green peas."

"Well, come, let's have lunch," our provider interrupted. "Shall we have it out or in?"

"Out," said Katherine.

V

The afternoon had flown. Kayding rode in from his pumping-plant at six o'clock (he was no eight-hour man) and I saw him up on the piazza waiting for the watchman's wife to call him in to dinner. She cooked for him; she had told me this and everything else about his housekeeping I wasn't ashamed to listen to, in the course of our laundry transactions. I wondered how much he could see of us as we went wandering about with Katherine between us admiring the camp and doting on the shore. She and I just then were on the brink of the cliff and she was eating one of the huge peaches Cecily had brought us, leaning over and wiping her fingers on a paper napkin. "What's one!" she cried; "I need a dozen—I need a sheet!" She squeezed the paper into a ball, and I as usual screamed: "Not on the beach! Whoever throws things over has to go down and pick them up."

"With pleasure, ma'am,"—and down she went;
it was the steepest part. She fluttered a hand up at me
gayly and cleared the trail in bounds and leaped into
the tall beach-grass at the foot of the cliff, then more
slowly through the soft sand and out to the surf's edge.
Her little figure was struck out against the west in a
dazzle of low sunlight; the sun sank into the fog-bank
and I saw her clear and sharp. She might have been
fourteen, in her straight skirt, hands resting on her
light hips, but no girl of that age would have stood
so long quietly gazing. One slender bird followed an
outgoing wave along the shine of the wet beach and
rose on thin, gray wings; Katherine looked up and
pointed, and we heard the cry of a lone curlew as
it vanished in the west. We had had curlews at Fort
Donelly; they migrated up the Snake River from the
Columbia and nested in the sage, one pair each year—
we had never seen more. Charley came out and stood
beside me. I had a caressed feeling, though he did not
touch me, as we looked down at our child.

"She'll like it," said he. "Did you see her go down
the path!"

"She always had those feet—with a sort of sense
in them.... Of course she'll like it; but that won't have
anything to do with her staying," I added bitterly. She
would love it all the more if she knew she could not
stay—and us, too, for that matter.

The figure of a man could be seen up there on the
empty piazza till dusk, a remarkable post of observation

where no one could call it prying; we were as open as the sky. Still, I was curious to know just how much he could see of us, our neighbor from his height. I had never been up there; yet it wasn't disturbing, somehow—he was that kind of a neighbor. You felt a trust in his private meditations as he lingered there till dark.

It was after ten o'clock, an uncanny hour for camp-folk, when we saw Katherine to her couch across tent-pegs and guy-ropes, her father carrying an acetylene lamp. He fastened it to the tent-pole on a level with our heads and withdrew to watch from outside the first illumination of the maiden-tent. Its new canvas walls took shadows startlingly.

"Ho," said he—"better set your lamp on the floor behind something; but see you don't knock it over or you'll have a smell."

"Aye, aye, sir!" said Katherine. "But why 'behind something'? I thought we were alone in this wide wilderness."

"Except Kayding and the watchman. We don't know all their lawful occasions around here after dark."

"Kayding-and-the-watchman," Katherine laughed. "Is that the name of thy servant the daddy calls a 'wild gazelle'?"

"He *has* got those eyes; but he's anything but wild. He's too tame, in fact."

"It's quite a name. Is it inseparable from 'watchman'?"

"Antonio Hernandez is the rest of it—two races struggling within him, and the American for all that is 'Tony.' But he's an utter dear!"

Katherine had opened her suit-case on her cot and sat there laying out her things; her dainty nighties that her own mother was a stranger to. I said they were too thin for camp, and she replied I needn't think I was going to put her into those "early Christian" ones that I wore, down to the wrist and up to the chin. (She had marked them as I was restoring a button and had smiled and said, "Mothers are so pathetic.")

"Well, go on about your Kayding. Where in the world did you pick him up?"

"He belongs here; he's our landlord by proxy. He could pack us off to-morrow if he chose, and he comes down as timid as a stray dog and we receive him as a favor. His father was a young Norse farmer and his mother—"

"Where do you get all this? It sounds made up."

"That much I got from him; but we can learn anything we want to know about anybody in Vallevista from the watchman's wife if I choose to gossip, or from an old man we talk to on the bench of his store. He told me one day, while Harvey went across the street for the mail, the whole story of a lawsuit. How the heirs of a Mr. Morehouse who owns this ranch have brought suit to prove him incompetent. He's seventy-five, but they can't wait for him to die. There are contracts expiring this year which they don't want him to renew. They have their own plans for managing the tract—thirty-six thousand acres. Quite a chore for an old man of seventy-five. They say he hasn't run it well, but it's something to run it at all. And the land is his own."

Katherine was rearranging the little piles of clothing on her bed. "I don't see how anybody can call thirty-six thousand acres of land his own unless he created it; even then it seems a want of imagination."

I dodged this ominous remark; for here at once we came upon one of our theoretical differences. My daughter's noble but depressing beliefs at this time had begun to verge on socialism in some of its alluring forms. What socialism is or may become, who can say; all I hoped was that I might not live to see it in practice.

There were various tuck-away places about the tent which the proud author of those places aspired to demonstrate. But my child, I saw, was now grown up.

"Leave those things alone, precious woman! Those are my every-day camp 'tockies you are hiding. Think I'm going to waste these on you and Dad?" She thrust out a silken ankle.

I told her I had noticed her 'tockies, and thought their quality rather good considering the size of her allowance.

"You may say so! Helen gave them to me. She got me lovely things in England—covered me with glory and shame! Look at that sweater!"

Helen was a cousin with whom Katherine had gone abroad, who took her, in fact, while we were helpless to do anything for our child. Not that we could have done that. Helen did whatever she pleased in such ways; in others—but that is her story. She was a little older than Katherine in years, decades older in experience of certain bitter, subtle kinds, the outcome of that story. There are sides and sides without doubt to this question of parents having their own way and will with their children's lives after they are past adolescence. If we could have had ours with Katherine, she would have missed altogether this modern friendship with Helen which I could see would be a prime factor in her life. It all came of their going abroad together, and that came of one talk they had when they first met (cousins can be strangers for years when one is an army-child and one a city-child) at a tea in New York when Katherine was taking a course in nursing leading to her Welfare Work. Not that they talked of that—Helen, be it said, was no more of a socialist than I am. I think she hoped the Welfare Work might wait a little at Katherine's age and with her type of mind, till she had seen a few other sides of life. And, with no illusions of her own on the subject, I know that Helen wished to see Katherine married—what, for her, would have to be broadly and very specially married. If that is to be "happily married."

"Where is a broom, please?" Katherine stood in the door of my tent after breakfast on a background of fog. "Or don't you sweep these mats?" My mats lay

outside face down on a clump of lupin bushes, the big
kind.

"You leave them alone when they aren't your
mats."

"Leave them for Harvey?" said the wily maiden.

I confessed that the tent-ladies did their own mats.
With mine I had a lazy way of dragging them along a
bank where the grass was clean and beating them on
their backs with her father's fire-stick, turning them
over and repeating the process. She waited till I had
finished.

"Give *me* the fire-stick and show me the bank."

"Oh, go on!" I said; but it ended in her doing my
mats and her own in no time; she was swift as light
about everything—this also was, I suppose, training.
She took all my chores into her competent hands,
but only that first morning. Equally quick she was to
see that I missed them, that she couldn't wait on me
without teasing me: I wanted to wait on her. I followed
her about like an old hen clucking. She may not have
cared for tea, camp-tea, but she allowed me to make it
for her, trotting back and forth between my own and
the cooktent and fussing over which cup and which
spoon she should use. She beamed on me and gave me
royal tips: sudden straight looks with her wonderful
smile that I knew had covered pain; little words and
inflections of her voice that had gained such subtlety!
She had the accent of cities; you couldn't interrupt her,
she was so brief. As a child it had been difficult to teach
her "manners"; now she had a manner which escapes

description, but to me was perfect rest. She had lived among nerves of the rich and uncontrolled emotions of the poor. She wasted no vital force of her own or that of others. The words were on my lips constantly as I watched her: "Let us lay aside every weight … and let us run with patience the race that is set before us." With patience! She was patient with her own mother, with my fondness and my yearning which she foresaw would cling, and threatened to hamper her. Her father yearned, too, but he did not cling. I spoke for him who would not ask for himself:

"Why not go fishing with them? I'm perfectly all right anywhere—I might even go myself!"

"Oh, bah—a man and his fish-pole! Three's a crowd." They understood each other. "We mustn't lose a minute of this summer, you and I. Every minute is lost when we're not together."

If she could say that (though I knew it was pure largesse) why did she add "this summer"!

I knew that I must hold hard against my passion of confirmed motherhood; it was no flare-up of kindling-stuff based on beauty's spell: Katherine was no beauty. All there was of me was in this altar-fire, the whole heap burning hard and strong. What could any living girl do with such mad mother-worship. It was the pain of knowing I must lose her that sharpened each moment spent together. There was nothing she said or looked or did that was not exquisitely adjusted to my tastes and senses and brain, except her "smoking," as I confessed, adding there ought to be another word for it when one's daughter did it.

"I'm not a slave to it," she assured me seriously. "'Shouldn't miss it here at all. But you want to know the worst:—I'll be seen as I am," screamed Mrs. Berry.'"

We laughed and let it go. She retained, however, the sense of my disapproval and showed it in little mischievous, deprecating ways, affecting defiance. My child was far the cleverer; she could do with me what she liked. As to the real question between us on which my life seemed to hang in those days, I covered it like a stolen nest. There were days and weeks before us in the immeasurable leisure of the camp, its casualness and its concentration, before I need speak, if I could bear the suspense.

We were seated in the shadow of the tent one afternoon quite late, I knitting, Katherine with a section of the morning paper hunting down scraps of war news, as we did daily. Harvey had passed us with his water-buckets; it was his time for going to the hotel.

Katherine sprang up: "I want to see where he gets the water."

"He gets it at Kayding's back door." She paused on the wing. "He's at home. I saw him ride in just now," I remonstrated.

"I'm not going to call on him. Doesn't Harvey go up every day?"

"But you don't, and I don't." I had followed her. "You'll frighten him to death."

"What an orphan child he must be. Let him hide, then!"

"There he is now." I halted.

"We can't turn back, mams; he's seen us."

He was coming to meet us. I was sorry for him. Katherine could not know how entrenched we were, each in our own defenses; he did not exist for her; she was treating him as if he were a pump.

He was coatless and hatless and rather untidy, a man just from his day's work. I could have wished his shirt had been cleaner and his hair not so long. The wind blew it the wrong way, an indignity his nice face bore with handsomely. And though he was distressed, I am sure, at his own appearance, he was not fussed by it, nor did he allow it to give an instant's pause to his greeting. That greeting was eloquent of his past, its loneliness and shyness and its gentleness and its pride. It held the charm, too, of that gazelle quality, the wildness that could never be roughness which my man had perceived. Well; if she couldn't see anything in him for the chance oddity of his exterior, I did not know our Katherine.

The tank-tower "stood up black" against the moorlands and the sky. We were on a platform beneath the square arch made by the bridge passageway that joined it to the hotel, in unavoidable intimacy with aged brooms and a plate of cat's food and flies, and a mop that even a Vallevista health-officer would have instantly condemned. Though why do I say Vallevista! Our own buckets of brown canvas did not look as clean

as we knew they were; each kitchen-door knoweth its
own bitterness—we had no business there! But as we
were there, uninvited, I sailed into the breach, leaving
Katherine to do her part of serene unconsciousness.

I asked Kayding where he lived, in this immensity
of floor-space and rows of windows. He pointed up
some outside stairs that needed sweeping to the corner
room above us, with windows east and west; he slept
up there; but when he offered to take me into his
living-rooms, I said we would wait and see the view
first while the sunset lasted. We had gained a much
higher ocean background by that climb of a hundred
feet or so; eastward beyond the moors, which cut our
own view, we could see now the whole valley beyond
and its sheltering hills, with old eucalyptus trees like
Japanese bronze in clumps on their brown slopes,
purple in shadow. And then I turned to satisfy my
curiosity about ourselves and how visible we were down
below. Katherine had already done so.

"Why, look at Us!" she cried. "Why, we're 'written
on the screen'!" She laughed up at Kayding who stood
beside her; he painfully changed color. This was all I
wanted to know, poor fellow: *he* was written on the
screen! He had not lost a minute of our show, it was
my conviction. A man socially more emancipated or
less sensitive might have laughed with Katherine—he
blushed. And I saw that he had scored with her in
that touch of embarrassment. He must have seen us
at our innocent meals out on the cliff, seen mother
and daughter strolling on the shore-path, watched

wistfully, perhaps, from his lonely eyrie our humble sparks of fire and candle-light hugged down by the shore. He would not have drawn near in the dark or taken any advantage, but the show had been free; he had, unavoidably almost, come to know us and our funny ways without intruding in any personal relation or taking the initiative involved in a "call." Who could say it wasn't natural and gazelle-like? But it made one's heart ache.

He took me through his kitchen-porch which seemed the nearer way to his sitting-room, dark and disorderly and as ugly as might have been supposed. I rather liked its odors of wood-smoke and tobacco and some of those shore-weeds that were stuffed into an atrocious vase in one corner. Outside the windows (unwashed for years) was all that view! It was all he had in fact. I examined a small set of book-shelves in the hope of something we could borrow; we were short of books. As we drank at his pump ("faucet," strictly speaking) and ate from his fields, begging a few books to read would not have cramped us, but there was not one I would have carried down the hill! When he had learned what was in my covetous mind, he offered me the key of "the doctor's house in town," he said. There was quite a little library there.

"But how about the doctor?" We had never heard of a doctor in Vallevista, though we trusted there was one.

He stared an instant. "The doctor," he said quietly, "is dead. Doctor Benedict Allen was my—almost my father. He adopted me; I grew up in his house—that house."

Here was gossip even the watchman's wife hadn't found time to tell me! She appeared to know so much, and was so more than ready to impart all she knew, that it was a little like listening at doors to permit her to get started. I hoped I had discouraged her somewhat. There was no help for my awkwardness; I hid my head in the books again.

"It would be nicer to have you with us when we break into your house."

"I should be very happy, but I have to go away soon for a few days. Have you heard of the lawsuit between Mr. Morehouse and his nephews, the heirs? I am one of the witnesses on his side. The case will be tried in San José." Here he offered me a key which he had hunted up while we were talking. "Any day when you are in town, please stop and help yourselves. The house is on Grove Street. I will speak to my aunt about your coming; she lives next door and looks after the place. She has a key, but this is simpler."

We were alone in the room. I asked him deliberately, to see if he had an opinion in the matter: "Do you mind being a witness in that suit? We have heard a little of what's said about it—just gossip."

"I hope the gossip is on his side. It ought to be. No; I'm glad to be his witness."

He was restless, longing to go back to Katherine whom he hadn't taken his eyes off of since we came up the hill. I have called him difficult to talk to; in her presence he became speechless like one hypnotized. When we went outside (Harvey had gone down with his pails), it was for me to take the lead in our own entertainment or we should have had to go too, and I wasn't ready. Kayding, poor wretch, was spell-bound. I asked where he grew the heliotrope he had brought us; where he had hidden it. He took us down the length of the fifty-foot piazza, as fast as we could drag Katherine away from the sunset.

"But this light can't last!" she cried.

While we lingered, a woman came slowly up the trail and turned into the road that ran beneath us. As we looked down she looked up and waved us a majestic greeting. We called her in camp "Mrs. Italy," or the "Purple Woman," for we never had seen her but in that one dress of faded purple heavy with damp, that clung to her hips and grand bosom. This was her hour, at low tide, to go down our path to the beach and out upon the uncovered rocks slippery with seaweed to gather limpets; such had been her errand to-night. She carried her pan on the palm of one hand held high on a magnificent bare, brown arm. And she walked a queen!

"Isn't she very tall for a Mexican woman?" Katherine inquired.

"When you see any one around here gathering limpets, to eat, you may know they're Portuguese," said Kayding disgustedly.

"She looks like one of the Immortals!" I cried. "No hungry generations tread *her* down."

"She has seven children and a husband and three dogs in one tent," Kayding chimed in with his antiphone, "and an acre of ground around her strewed with rags and scraps of her scarecrow housekeeping. She's the laziest woman of the whole bunch."

Our dispute brought beams of mirth to Katherine's eyes.

"But she's beautiful!" said I. "Look at the mist on her hair—sculped hair; the wind can't stir it."

"Stiff with grease," Kayding responded. His eyes besought Katherine's: "Do *you* call her handsome?"

A man that grows heliotrope and waits to exhibit it has no use for Purple Women whom he knows too well—and "hungry generations" were to him unborn, one might say. I had no business to cut him out of the conversation with such allusions. Usually he took these speeches of mine with a modest deference that put one to shame, but to-night he was plainly not himself; our talk baffled him and made him uneasy.

"This lady"—Katherine indicated me mockingly—"thinks we are a skinny lot, we Americans 'straight'; she thinks we need such aliens as that one, to improve our looks as a nation."

It was a remark that cut both ways: whether we classed him ourselves as another "alien" or so little regarded him as to forget that he was an alien in every drop in his veins—equally he was not of us. And it hurt. He must have heard many times in the village speech those slurs, "Dago," "Portugee," "Mex."—all were as one to the Americans "straight" of Vallevista. Americans like Mr. Hoadley from Missouri.

It was altogether a despairing visit, starting wrong and going from bad to worse. But we still had the garden.

He took us around the hotel and down a short path to a hollow where his little treasure lay lapped from the north winds. Yes; he did have something else besides his view—it was a lovesome little garden; you could see what hours of devotion had been spent there. Against a low wall on the southern side his midsummer flowers were still blooming, white lilies standing tall amidst dahlias just coming on in a riot of colors (I should have put them in a different place). The heliotropes lived retired in a shady corner, much petted evidently, but every flower was gone. He had picked his last for us.

He passed a hand caressingly amongst the leaves. "I'm sorry —!"

"Ser Federigo and his falcon," I murmured to Katherine.

She looked away from me. We were doing our best to earn each other's disapproval, but I bore off the palm!

"You stripped it for us," I reminded Kayding; "and there's the last of it!" Katherine wore a withered sprig hanging from her buttonhole, *not* a proof of her attachment to it, merely she hadn't noticed it was there.

"Oh, you mustn't, mustn't cut those lilies!" I cried; "we've nothing to put them in but our water-pitchers. No, no; they're too lovely just there. Please!—or we shall have to run home before we rob you any more."

Aside from the signs of work and constant attendance the garden had an unpremeditated look that was one of its charms; except in the case of a great, sprawling geranium that held the center of the stage, its fierce scarlet spoiling all the colors near it.

"I'd like to throw that fellow out," Kayding apologized, "but I found it here; it was the only thing I had at first. I keep it for that and because it put up such a good fight here all alone."

A hoot from camp warned us that supper waited. Kayding was asked to return our visit, but I am apt to put too much emphasis on an invitation that I've had on my conscience—I asked him to dinner.

"Do come; any night. Come Sunday. Sunday is our show night, because of spick-and-span dish-towels. We don't eat them, but we use them as holders; all our skillets have aluminum handles and—we are served out of skillets!"

Katherine's eyes shed mirth, but our host remained perfectly grave. He might have been standing at attention listening to orders.

"I shall be very happy to dine with you, but not so soon as Sunday. I have to go to San José for a few days," he mentioned, precisely as if he hadn't already told me not ten minutes before. I abased myself with futile apologies.

"And the key?" He offered it once more. I had forgotten it, laid it down. The key of his friend's house who was dead, his almost father! I accepted it, re-accepted it, humbly, and we went down the hill.

"What do you think of your 'Americans straight'?" I asked Katherine as she slipped her hand through my arm, "We're a tactful breed, aren't we?"

"I saw you were playing a desperate game, but I don't know *what* you're doing with that man's key?"

"Key! It's more like a coal of fire. I broke into his life just now without any key, and he's presented me with his whole past—not once, but twice! I laid it down and forgot it and he gave it again."

"He'd give you his head if you intimated you could use it. You've bewitched him. He'll never get over this summer."

"He never will, but not because *I've* bewitched him."

"Daddy fishes and you hunt big game," she went on teasing.

As the path narrowed she dropped behind and I heard her singing lightly to herself:

"We'll chase the antelope over the plain,
The wild gazelle we'll bind with a chain,—"

"'The tiger's cub,'" I corrected.

"The tiger's cub we'll bind with a chain,
And the wild gazelle—"

"What about the 'wild gazelle'?"
"—'With his silvery feet, I'll tame for thee, a
playmate sweet,'" I finished.

"Sure!" said Katherine delightedly. "A Victorian
ballad—they had to break loose somehow. I wonder
where you got your common sense? And yet you were
made of it!"

"I and Byron were not contemporaries, you
know," I protested. "That was one of my mother's
songs—she that was a Quaker lady!"

"How gorgeous," said Katherine. "Did she sing
'The Pirate's Serenade'?"

"She did—to her babies. And liked it as much as
they did."

"Byron didn't write those things, though?"

"It was the Byron craze produced them, I
suppose."

"*He's* perfectly Byronic," she said; "and you're in
between, and so you have the worst of it. But you've
done for him. He's bound with a chain. And now what
are you going to do with him?"

"Don't you want him—for a 'playmate sweet'?"
With these words, jarred out of me, I sat down
suddenly on the path—not hurt in the least. Katherine
pounced down beside me full of remorse, and we
both sat there and laughed immoderately. It gave her
the chance of her life, though, to mock me of my pet

vanity. "I *swear* I don't lose my footing once in a year!" said I. But thereafter I was her "wild gazelle" with "slippery" feet, and poor Kayding had a little peace. Indeed, after that preposterous visit, and after our visit to the doctor's house (his past), she forbore, I noticed, to joke about him.

VI

Sunday was a day fit for divine festivals and sacrifice to the high gods. Never in Vallevista had we seen such a sky, Emerson's "blue urn of fire." I said to Charley, after breakfast, "What is the use of all this shilly-shallying. Why don't we show Katharine the Point?"

"Why don't we!" he smiled. "It's up to you."

It was not our camp custom to go fishing on Sunday. Sunday mornings Harvey religiously boiled the inescapable dish-towels and performed other rites of that nature in the cook-tent, necessitating a fire. Hence chowder, which needs long cooking, was the chef's particular Sunday dish. I wounded him by proposing we should go early and lunch at the Point, so Katherine might see it by morning light; the western sun would be in our faces all the afternoon.

"What, no chowder!"

That settled it: we spent the morning in camp and I fortified my spirit with chowder, though in fact I could not eat…. I was breathless as a lover, keeping pace with my girl's long, light stride through the sweet-smelling fields, getting up my speech and my courage to make it; and Katherine preserved the orthodox air of feminine unconsciousness of what was coming, but I think she knew why I could not walk fast that day without panting. Once she put her arm suddenly and strongly around me, but we said nothing.

She was ready with all the praise we could have asked. I should have been happier with less: it would have promised better if she had been critical, asked questions and demurred a little at this or that. She stood on Cortez's rock, her father beside her, his arm through hers, his big-booted feet planted next her slender, supple ones that took such firm hold. The wind beat back her skirts as she faced it—the west wind which is the wind of adventure and purpose and longing, and the way, I said to myself, of partings between us and them, the generations that go and stay. They might have stood so for the Future and the Present, a very stanch and solid present with a calm, far-sighted eye fixed on the horizon. He was searching it for a steamer's smoke; there was nothing in sight—not a sail, and landward, not a house; but yes—the hotel! and its one occupant. Tony Kayding in our cosmos stood for humanity. As a social outlook for a girl like Katherine, it might have seemed a trifle restricted. But she had the realm of beauty, of spiritual vastness and peace; and as all the winds of heaven would be free to visit her, so would the soul-currents of the universe. She could keep her world-consciousness; no form of communication but the personal, the tangible, would be denied her; she was herself the most intangible thing alive. Nor could I believe she would ever cease to be a "child of the heather and the wind."

The men went away out of sight to their fishing-rock; we saw no more of them, only the tips of two fish-poles dipping and rising against the sea's expanse. Katherine and I found a sheltered cleft and we sat there cushioned on mesembryanthemum, as on beds of amaranth and moly. The flowers were few and discolored, and the fat, three-sided leaves tipped with crimson hinted the summer was passing.

"Why were you afraid to bring me here? Afraid I wouldn't like it? We always like the same things—it's a heavenly place."

"Well," said I, "does that mean it would suit us!"

"It's a place where it is 'always afternoon.'" She let her voice linger on the words caressingly, but not hopefully to my ear.

"It's 'afternoon' with us."

"Are you so sure? I shouldn't think dad would be."

"You mean the war? Washington will keep us out of it. It maddens him to think of it. He must get to work at something active." I laid before her a few of our surface plans; the site of the house, the garden, the water-system, the horse- and cow-pasture. There was no life in them to her ear—nor to mine, any longer.

"Horses? Then you will ride again?"

"I ride!"

"I can see it, for him," said Katherine after a silence; "but less so for you, somehow."

"You might say that of every home we've ever had. Yet they were homes."

"Ah; I should say! But there was virtue in that necessity. There's no necessity for virtue now; this home should be your reward."

"But, child! What do you think I deserve?"

"Of course it's wonderful—to be so far away from all the suffering. None of us kids deserve that. Only those who have suffered their share—had the hand of fate upon them."

"You're not talking of me! I haven't suffered my share—or, yes; it was my share!" I added to myself. A woman who has lost one child through ignorance and spoiled another's life through vanity may be said to have suffered—not her share, perhaps, but her due. She has no claims to exemption.

"Mams, dear," said Katherine, more lightly, seeing the look on my face, "haven't you been in love with places before? Little heavens you and dad discovered and had to leave behind you? Wasn't that part of the charm—knowing they were not for keeps? Would you miss that, I wonder, if it were for keeps, and you found yourselves anchored?"

I answered listlessly that I had flirted with places before, but now I was ready to marry and settle down.

"I'd sign the deeds to-morrow and marry this, if we could get it."

"But why have deeds? Then your troubles would begin, it seems to me. You practically own it now, as long as you can trail down here and sit on it like this. What could be better than this?"

"Summers, perhaps; but how about winters, and old age?"

"You are not old; but when you are you'll need a different kind of home, won't you?"

"Don't you say that!"

She looked at me quickly, understandingly. "I know you'll never coddle yourselves. But I want you nearer—where I could come and coddle you whenever I feel like it and you can stand it."

That was enough; I had her answer. What could we expect? If she had been married, we should not have planned to attach her and enclose her life in ours; we were not physically dependent on her ministrations to our wants. She was young and she was free; it was not afternoon with her.

"I can't seem to see you and dad spending your last days here; they won't be so few. And you're nice folks." She coaxed me with her smile. "You ought to be with other nice folks in cities. You love the big world— you're a gay little talker. How are you going to bear it, for years and years—this silence, and the sea?"

"I'll talk to the sea," said I, choking a little, and turning away.

She brought her cheek close to mine with her arm around me. We seldom kissed—we rubbed cheeks like horses. Hers had its own sweetness, which wasn't youth nor health nor sachets nor sanctity, but made of them all and blessed with a mother's memories of the babies she had bathed and kissed in the backs of their necks, and the hollows of their feet and hands. I felt as if I breathed the soul of her through its thin tenement. But she wasn't mine, even if I had bathed her as a baby.

"Don't pretend to me that you're afraid of silence! You know this silence feeds the best kind of talk, the kind we might have. Would I miss the world if I could have you?"

"You know I could say the same—if I dared."

It was time now to ease the decision for her; I changed the subject.

"Speaking of bearing things—how do you suppose Cecily manages to bear what she has to put up with right along? How does she?"

"Rather well, I think, on the whole. She doesn't talk."

"Not to you?"

"Not a word, directly. Cecy, you know, is not so exacting as we are in some ways; in others more so. Her world is with her a good deal; it's a world where one's cars are clean. That's mean of me, but she is ours, she's Us. It's nice to be more than one kind of a family. We couldn't spare Cecy's daintiness; it's a quality in itself. She's a beautiful person, and she might have no more sex than a flower for all the danger there is in her beauty, for her or for any one else. It seems to have played her that one trick, luring Peter. That's enough!"

"She strikes me as growing a little hard."

"Yes; one isn't surprised when she asserts there are no happy marriages but old ones where they've spent years on the job—you and dad, for example. She didn't say that! … The little boys came back from the other grandmother's the day before I left. Great little chaps. She's doing wonderfully well with them, I think."

"How much does she have a chance to do? Mrs. Dalbert is an overpowering sort of person. The children are all Dalbert in her eyes."

"Cecy will stand up for her own when it's the children," said Katherine. "Madam Dalbert knows she can't go too far or Cecily will leave Peter. I suppose there's no doubt the law would give her the children."

"You did not speak of that!"

"Not a word. Madam Dalbert brought the boys and stayed to luncheon. I thought she seemed rather fond of Cecily."

"Not proud of her, however."

"Well, she can't be proud of her own son."

"Did you see anything of Peter?"

"He took me motoring once. He drives like a madman, but extremely well. He wanted to try my nerve; exactly like a brutal sort of boy. And he came into Cecily's box one night when she was giving a little theater-party for me. He wasn't at our dinner, but he had perceptibly 'dined.'"

"Not enough to do; never obliged to do anything he didn't want to right along without stopping. Really, Mr. Dooley has said it once for all, the truth about education."

"We talked a great deal about that, Cecy and I, more than about anything else. She is keen for the best that is being done in that way. Children are my hobby, you know."

She said this quite casually, as though I must have been aware of the fact. I had never dreamed of it. "I don't think much of children as a hobby," said I, sinking into bitterness. "I like children as just children, my own or anybody's."

"But there are the children who aren't anybody's. Some one has to look after them."

"It should be women who haven't children of their own, or women who have embraced a future that is sure to be childless. Is that the case with you, dear?"

"I haven't sworn it," said Katherine, smiling. "Such women as you speak of can hardly be young—I mean the childless kind. Isn't the very youthfulness of the younger ones, isn't their faith and physical strength and even their ignorance a rather good thing? All real mothers begin young. Of course it's wonderful," she repeated, gazing off at the long restful shore-line, "to feel one's self exempt. But if we go anywhere near it, if we let it touch us, it's a sure hold. You're never able to say you are free, again."

That ended our argument. I had my answer, and the day was lost. I still clung to my old belief in those ties that God decreed to bind. But I saw where I failed, even in my own eyes, in selfish isolation. The families that believe most in the ties that bind include the Neighbor. Katherine's neighborhood had increased in size, that was all. But it made all the difference between her dream of life and mine.

At bedtime that night I broke a scheme to her father which had been hatching in my mind. "Wouldn't it be good to see Katherine on a horse again! Do you think you could manage it? I could borrow a saddle and habit from Cecily."

"I suppose we might hire something on three legs," he answered without enthusiasm. "Do we need horses and a car?"

"I didn't say horses. And there's only one decent road to motor on—it goes nowhere into the heart of things. There are those lovely cañons back of us! I wonder if Kayding could help you find a horse for her?"

"He has a horse—but they're not easy to hire, decent ones. He would offer her his and hire a screw for himself. Do you want to get in as deep with him as that?"

"We could make it up to him."

"How?"

"By letting him ride with Katherine."

I was in bed and he in his pyjamas stood waiting to put out the light. He looked hard at me and remarked cryptically (but I can't pretend to have missed his meaning), "If you want to punish him for anything, why, go ahead, but if you care a cent's worth for the poor devil, I'd leave it alone."

I didn't leave it alone. I wanted Katherine to know the country intimately, to be "intrigued" with it, to see it with the eyes of one who knew its realities and its people, and who was one of them himself and who loved it like a son. We had not asked for realities; we were spectators; we were there for utterly selfish reasons, to find some substitute for life. It could not, I acknowledged, be enough for her: the shore-paths and the sunsets and the ground-swell rolling in on our laughter and our dreams and idle talk. It was a pagan scheme of existence on the background of the war. But show her the human, the seamy side of this earthly paradise—the tent-family of our Purple Woman as it were (imagine the state of her babies!). If she was pledged to work for other people's babies why not do it here? The opportunities for it were vague, to me, but the needs must be acute. And Kayding would know what they were.

It might bring him suffering (though in my opinion it was already too late to spare him that), but our girl would give him more than she would cost him. She would show him "stars he never saw before"; and if she left him with "divine regrets" they might be his salvation from infinitely meaner regrets and poverty of life and a marriage that would drag him down. I had it all plotted out as to the future. It was his fate to know one girl like her. I foresaw he would take the shaping of the Lord's hand upon him like the patient, incorruptible soul I believed him to be, and I wished him well of his ordeal; but also I couldn't spare him.

VII

We went to Kayding's (or the doctor's) house on
Monday; this is going back on my tale a little. We
shamelessly opened his front door and walked in and
began our search for something to read. Our sense of
the humor of the proceeding saved it somewhat from
pure grotesqueness and bald intrusion. It was a little
old adobe house on a side street set in a garden choked
with overgrown shrubbery. A great rose-climber went
up the front gable to the roof—there was no second
story—darkening the rooms within. They were all small
rooms and had a long-shut-up smell. The first one we
entered would have been the waiting-room, and a door
opposite the front door led into the doctor's study;
but we opened by mistake a door on the left which
disclosed what must have been the operating-room.
The study crossed both these rooms with windows at
each end, and it had a fireplace sufficient for the needs

of the climate. The bookshelves ran all along one side filling the space between two doors into the waiting- and the operating-rooms. There were professional-looking charts and portraits cheaply framed above the books, also a glazed bookcase which held the doctor's technical library. A table stood in front of the hearth, long and narrow like the room, and a worn leather chair stood near it as if shoved back by some occupant who had just risen. Every part of the house needed cleaning yet the atmosphere though mummified was not unpleasant. Our own sensations, as we stood there and looked about us, were rather so.

"I think this is going pretty far, don't you?" asked Katherine. She spoke as if a sick person lay in the next room.

"Well, we're in for it," I replied. A slow, heavy step could be heard coming through the back part of the house: "That must be the aunt."

The door opened, and it was the aunt no doubt, an old Mexican woman, not so old, perhaps, as she appeared in her unresisting, messy way. Very dark, very fat, dressed in dark cotton clothes as if to save washing—everything on her needed it, I am sure. Yet in five minutes she had us smiling, hanging on her every word. I can't pretend to spell her accent, and of course one cannot spell a voice.

"These are the ladies Antonio tell me is coming?" she addressed us, looking from me to my daughter, but returning to me. "How sorry I am I have not clean up! I did not know you be here so—" politeness

forbade her to finish the sentence. We certainly had
been "soon."… "Now I shame!" We smiled and she
laughed softly with raised eyebrows of deprecation.
"It was the books he say you like to look at. Ah, they
have not been touch for years—years! It is too bad you
find them all dusty like that. Some books, ain't it! She
chuckled as she drew her finger along their backs. "All
belong to Antonio, an' the 'ouse an' the little one in the
back of the yard. I take care of both houses, but I too
ole, too lazy. 'Tonio he never get mad—he don' know
how! Tha's like hees mother. I was her aunt, sister to
her grandfather's brother what married her great-aunt.
'Tonio is my baby since she die. An' 'before, two years,
she was too seeck to do anything for him, an' it won' be
safe the doctor tell her because she have the trouble in
her chest. She cough. Oh, he was an angel, that doctor!
Doctor Benedict Allen—Was 'Tonio telling you about
him?

"See; look in here!" She threw open the door
between the book-shelves and showed us the bare,
dusty room we had glanced into, with the operating-
table under the keen light of a curtainless window.
"That where his father die. They bring him here to the
doctor, the men what he go shooting with. He killed
himself with his own gun. Yes; it was accident: they
was good men. Twenty-eight years, an' a wife an' a baby
coming an' some rent he owe on his land that year.
So that was a bad Sunday shooting for Maria. Only
for Doctor Allen she never go through with it. But he
was an angel! Never one bill he send her all what time

he take care of her an' give her wine an' medicine an' wegetable when she could n' eat. An' tell her how it is bad for 'Tonio if he sleep with her; an' he fin' out about me an' go himself to San José to get me. I never see San José again, but I was willing—more, more than willing. For I love Maria an' the boy like my own. Not many people come to see me an' I don' talk to nobody. But I know Antonio have great opinion of these ladies," she singled me with a slight inclination tactfully as the older woman, "or he don' give his key! I never knew him do that before.... You will please lock the door when you go out, ladies; an' don' make haste. Stay as long as you like to." She rose and we rose and shook hands. But still she lingered.

"Now, let me tell you—*I* don' talk to nobody. But I want you to see how that was about Doctor Benedict—we always call him so. He was coming every day at the last; an' she was getting weaker; an' that day she have 'Tonio at the bedside looking at him an' her hand on his curls. An' the doctor was seeing what she had in her heart, the pain to leave him, five years old.

"'Will you give him to me, Maria?' he says. 'Will you trust him to me like my own son? I would like to keep him with me and leave him all I have.'

"I thought she would have say 'yes' with one sob out of her heart, but she wait a little before she answer. 'When I married my husband we say, if our children are girls they shall belong in my church, but if we have a son he can do what way he think best—can choose his own religion. I think you are the best man in the

world, Doctor Benedict,' she says, 'but no man can
be perfect unless he got religion.' She wait an' in a
moment she get more strength. 'You won' *put anything
in the way* if 'Tonio should *want* his mother's religion?'

"'No,' he says; 'what kind of a man would I be if I
did that! It shall be left to his own conscience.'

"'When he have one,' she say. Then he say he try
to see that he does have a conscience about everything
what makes religion—the name of it he can choose for
himself.

"That don' satisfy her, but she can't talk no more.
By and by, 'Thank you,' she say. 'You have been father
an' mother an' brother to me.' An' that was the last. An'
I think he would have been more than that, but she
was too seeck. I think Doctor Benedict was in love with
Maria, but only as a good man. The best that ever lived.
Some folks try to make a talk about his taking her son,
but they can't make that go—not here! Nobody could
stay in this town an' say such thing about Doctor Allen.
She was just one little woman what always stay at
home; they don' know her, but everybody know him.

"When you go out, ladies, will you please to watch
that cat next door? He want to get in here all the time;
he hide under the rosebush. Would you please to shut
the gate queeck! He eat all the nice singing-bird in the
garden an' he never catch a rat, not if you throw it at
his head."

"Well; there was a man who did not miss his
opportunity," said Katherine.

"I feel as if he were here in the room with us."

"Why not Maria?"

"He must have had the personality that would 'come back.' She had temperament I suppose; and eyes—gazelle eyes, and gave them to her son. He's what daddy calls pure mongrel, but he's remarkably pure. And the doctor, you see, kept him out of the streets."

"We are in his house," Katherine reminded me briefly.

"We won't stay if you really disapprove of me. There won't be any fun in it."

"We have taken his key; can we hand it back without using it?"

"*I* took it—I'm always taking people's keys and getting too deep into their lives."

We felt each other's critical presence rather more, perhaps, than the actual indecency of our research, digging there among the ashes of the dead; still it was interesting. Doctor Allen's books showed the choice of a good American and a particularly good Californian, but it was a curiously limited collection and in the literary sense not a reader's library. There was a great deal of Americana relating to the Pacific Coast, its Native Races and its Discoverers, and their wars of possession and dispossession. Much about the gold-rush and the exploits of the forty-niners; Frémont's planting the flag treated in the spirit of the time, nothing as to the ironic side of that conquest till we came to a book I had glanced over at Cecily's called "The Beginnings of San Francisco," an apparently fair, but not always flattering, record somewhat loosely put together. Much about the Missions and the work of the padres;—the only novels were "Ramona," and "Uncle Tom's Cabin!" There was no poetry whatever, not even Joaquin Miller; but there was everything that has ever been printed by or relating to Luther Burbank, evidently a worshiped enthusiasm.

I said to Katherine it was the most monkish set of books one could imagine and without a scrap about religion amongst them. She asked what I meant by that.

"It leaves out the Tender Passion as if it didn't exist. Of course you can't have poetry without it."

"Are you looking for it?" she inquired *à la* Doctor Johnson.

"I'm looking for Bret Harte and Mary Austin and Norris and Stoddard and a few other rather notable Californians. In such a state-proud collection I can't see why they aren't here, unless there's a method in it. If you cut out everything emotional, erotic, why, there you are! And there you have the boy who grew up on it—cloistered, a mass of fuel and not one spark. What a quaint doctor—a genius! I adore the man."

"Then why undo his work?" Katherine asked with startling perspicacity.

"Because it's time," said I, "if the boy is ever to be a man."

"Oh, for Heaven's sake —!" She did not finish.

VIII

Kayding came to dinner on the following Sunday. He said nothing about his week in court until asked how the case was going, when he replied that it seemed to be going well for Mr. Morehouse. Charley alluded to the general opinion that the tract had gone to the dogs pretty much, which rather tended to preserve some of its most attractive features.

Kayding said: "He's never been equal to managing it, but he wasn't any more so twenty years ago when he sent for the mother of these men, because she was his sister, and a widow poorly off. He brought them all out here and looked after them. I think they are curs to sue him. If he's incompetent to manage this land, they are too mean to be trusted with it."

"You must have been a rather good witness," I remarked.

Kayding gave me a preoccupied look and went on fixedly. "I am taking Mr. Morehouse's orders every day, now, while he's called senile. He put in the irrigation work here without any advice, except mine. The ditches leak"—he smiled at my husband—"but the crops look fairly well. He hasn't many friends; most of the testimony against him was pure gossip."

"Such as what?" said I, who love gossip in spite of my family's disapproval.

"They say that with land enough for a British duke he doesn't own even a Ford—drives the same old horse and buggy he's had for fifteen years; has his boots re-soled, and his wife does her own work. She's hard to get on with—no one can stay with her. That's not his fault, and perhaps it isn't hers altogether. They call *me* a 'nut' because I choose to live out here alone with a house standing empty in town." He turned to us, to Katherine, shyly.

"You saw my Aunt Luisa?" Answering his own question, he added, "She was very happy over your call, only the house wasn't dusted! She hopes you will come again."

We replied that we would, and we had had a very nice time with his Aunt Luisa.

"*She* loves gossip," he smiled, apologizing. No doubt Aunt Luisa had given him a detailed report of our visit which would have included a confession of her own loquacity; but if he was a little ashamed of it, he was not ashamed of her. "I knew she would have to tell you about my mother and Doctor Allen. It is the whole of her life; and she can't help bragging about the house, though she refuses to live in it. Did she tell you about Mr. Morehouse and the land? ... She will—the next time."

Kayding seemed a trifle more awakened, stirred, perhaps, by his week in a city of some size and his contact with the wits of lawyers. It must have been quite a moving experience in the current of his existence. Something would come of it—something had come of it: an active sense of injustice, a strong indignation against those who couldn't wait, who would snatch an old man's last crumb of life, and from the hand that had fed them. Mr. Morehouse seemed another instance of the friendless rich, envied and plundered by his own kin who had less than kindness for him. Kayding himself supplied the story which Aunt Luisa had omitted in the course of her reminiscences. He told us Mr. Morehouse never had asked a penny's rent, since his father's death, for the few acres the widow needed around her house, and he had remitted the rent that was over-due on the ranch, which had been re-let, but the widow's field remained practically her own till she died.

"It wasn't much to him, but it was a great deal to her. And that is another reason why I was glad to be on his side. He isn't a generous man—he isn't much of a man, anyhow; but he doesn't cheat if he knows it. And if he holds on to more than he can do with, how many would give it up in his place?"

"I wonder what we'd do if we had it!' Katherine spoke, glancing at me. "What would you do, mams?"

"Burn down that hotel before I slept a wink."

"What would you put in its place?" Kayding inquired.

"Nothing. My husband wouldn't allow me, of course, but I should like to do just as your ancestors did: let it all lie as Nature made it, with flocks and herds roaming over it and plenty of horses to ride."

"'We'll chase the antelope over the plain,'" Katherine murmured, twinkling at me.

"And what would *you* do?" Kayding turned to her with visible effort in meeting her eyes.

Katherine was very lovely that night. I had insisted on a white skirt and a different sort of blouse; I was tired of mannish collars and four-in-hands. Her blouse to-night was open at the throat and a thin silver chain with a gleaming bead here and there trickled down the front of it. She sat on the edge of Harvey's cot which was modestly covered with white canvas. Harvey (not at our suggestion) waited on us, and Kayding was in his seat next the stove. He had dressed for the occasion, mistakenly, of course. One could see he was miserable in his starched shirt and vest and all. He suffered from Katherine's eyes opposite and from the stove behind: between the two fires it was an occasion that called for gallantry. He did well. But it was another of those ordeals he owed to me, and which I am bound to witness did not find him wanting in the spirit and the humility of a gentleman.

"Are we talking sense or nonsense?" Katherine asked, postponing her answer to his question.

"Both," said I.

"Well, if there must be houses, I would build a big one, big enough to hold not one family, but an idea."

"Oh, don't be goody-goody! Spare us your philanthropies. We're out for 'the fun of the road,' as Mr. Hoadley says."

"What I see," Katherine emphasized, looking me down, "is a great school, but more than a school—not philanthropic—very expensive; the rich girls should make it pay so well that poor ones might come without pay. Beautiful buildings just to fit the shore; a farm and dairy and a garden, and a hospital—where some of the girls might train;—I shall not pinch myself! There would be girls of any age after they can leave their mothers and learn how to be mothers themselves."

"It's a mercy there are to be a few mothers!" I interrupted.

"And hostesses and great ladies, and small ladies, and just plain women. Teachers of all kinds and all sexes, even the 'third sex'"—she flipped this at me with another twinkle. "Sport of all kinds, horses, of course— antelopes if mamma insists. Everything in work or play that can make a girl fit and manly."

Kayding looked distressed: "'Manly'?" he repeated helplessly. "Is it a school for any special work?"

"No," said Katherine. "They would be girls of all work that they could do well; but no concessions to their being 'only girls'—and no swank on that account either. 'I would have my daughters to be valiant and brave men.'"

"Those aren't her words," I reassured Kayding, who gasped in silence. "Katherine's only copying. The 'daughters' of St. Theresa lived—how long ago, Katherine? When did your cult begin?" I hadn't helped the matter for Kayding.

"Start something easier," Charley requested. "Mr. Kayding has been with lawyers all the week. If the ranch belonged to me, Kayding, I tell you what I'd do, even before I tore down the hotel. Build a road with culverts. Why do you let your fanners turn their ditches into the roads?—if you call 'em roads."

"Because the roads cross the fields, by permission, where the water has to go."

The retort was acclaimed with laughter. Kayding by his color grew hotter—I glanced at Charley.

"Will you permit us to smoke, ladies New and old?" he smiled at Katherine. "Or shall we go outside?" The "ladies" rose and we all went outside, and one of the ladies accepted a light from her father and joined the smokers. It was, I thought, a mercy perhaps to Kayding—that touch destructive of moon-magic—despairingly lovely as she looked. It destroyed nothing for me, though, and I am a hater of the practice for my "sex" as I am of several more of our rights that are manifest enough—and that also begin with the letter "s."

I have made an event, or a circumstance, of that supper, small and queer as it was. We had no events in common with Kayding that were not small and queer. I had now worked out my riding scheme, conscientiously opposed (and naturally) by her father. He hated to "use" our neighbor, and he hated the appearance of intimacy which would result from his riding with Katherine; which we knew would follow. Katherine herself resisted a little at first.

"What do you want to put me on a horse for? *You* don't want to ride, old dad! Though it would be mighty good for you. I've had all the riding that belongs to one girl and *I* don't need to keep down my flesh." This was the manner of her protest, but the light was in her eye, and she looked like her young-girl self once more when she slipped into Cecy's cross-saddle habit and tightened her long, pale braids. The watchman, always convenient, we subsidized as a stable-man and Kayding had reacted according to prophecy. Only the horse he hired for himself did not appear to be a screw. His own, he said, was safer on a trail and they meant to do some climbing. The light was in his eye too.

Katherine's father looked at me sternly as they first rode off together, watched by us in silence. "I hope you know what you're doing? I'm darned if I know!"

"I don't do anything. I just experiment. Things work out of themselves."

"That's how the boy experimented when he held his sister's wax-doll to the fire. He wasn't the fire!"

"Well, then, I *am* the fire; mothers are one of the incalculable forces of nature, I won't deny it."

"I guess that's why Katherine wants a few manly mothers in her scheme. Do you know any father who would do this?" He nodded at the figures growing distant in the dust.

"Yes; a father in a novel that you've never read,—a philosopher, with a tragedy in his life. He made more tragedy because he didn't stop in time. His experiment was a perfect success, only he carried it too far."

I admitted to myself it was a desperate deed. There are many things about that summer which I don't pretend to explain or excuse. It was a time of transition and suspense, and states of mind—because we didn't know the ground under our feet. The war—which we did not talk of—kept my husband in a fever, as I knew; I was nervous on his account. And the spreading peril abroad seemed reflected microscopically in our own family affairs; doubts about Cecily, longings for Katherine—to have her for a little while, before the massed opinions and emotions of the city swallowed her up. We were transfixed, both nationally and individually, in a nightmare of helplessness. And the whole human world looking to us in our safety, asking but for a word—if that were all—to say if we were on any side but our own.

IX

It was past the middle of August with September
creeping upon us. We had no reason to suppose
Katherine had altered her purpose. I could scarcely bear
her out of my sight unless the sacrifice meant a greater
happiness to her. That happiness poor Tony was giving
her. I watched it go on—I who had never forgiven
Mrs. Dalbert what I called her treachery about Peter!
But I said to my conscience, "Pain means growth and
sensibility; he will be the richer for this ploughshare.
He isn't cheating himself and he can't have any hopes
that can delude him now or in the future. And
Katherine will not delude him. She will play fair."

More than four years we had been parted from
our girl: her two years at Bryn Mawr, before we were
sent to the Philippines, another two years while we
were there which completed her course, and the year
abroad with Helen—the rest she had done for herself.

She used to come into our tent after the evening rides, take my camp-chair beside her father while I lay on my cot and watched her. Stretched back with her hands clasped behind her head, the wind-roughened braids I loved worn in that girlish club, legs in riding-boots crossed, a cigarette, "I shame" to say, between her lips—she would cock her eye at me saucily and put on a delicately practiced air for pure swagger. A boy in her attitudes and as careless of pose; Greek in her long, smooth limbs and beautifully finished head, modern to the last word in her clear-cut face and vivid expression, terse and significant in speech, or slangy or both—she was the offspring of our hearts' blood, I might say— and our various odd homes and enforced conditions. And now I wanted to stop the clock, "nail the wild star in its track on the half-climbed zodiac"... Ah, my wild star, my darling.

So they rode, evening after evening, between Tony's early supper and our tent-dinner to match. What sunsets they must have seen, what planets in the west, what gray, soft dusks struck through with growing moonlight, or nights of stupendous splendor when the light flaming from sky to shore called us out to look and cry aloud; wonderful signaling, the West bidding the East good-night and the East repeating the word in melancholy. And down the long beaches that endless roll of surf. Up in the hills they could not hear it, but they would have a silence that might be even better. I wondered if there was anything they could say to each other, those two!

When they were later than usual I would go out and watch for them, and see them on the moor-line, perhaps, their shapes dark against the sky, and wait for them to come pelting down and swing their horses on our little terrace behind the tents. Tony would drop off and stand at Katherine's stirrup—I knew that she did not require his hand or his help; she humored him as one would a shy, hampered boy; one wanted to give him a chance to express himself somehow.

I said to Katherine one day, quite off-handish, though I quaked a little:

"I've sent for Tennyson for Tony; I want him to read 'Locksley Hall.'"

"For goodness' sake, why?"

"Because he's just the age for it, and the background is this place exactly. He hears us go on with our lingo:—'dreary gleams about the moorland'—it's a shame to leave him out of it. It's unmannerly."

"He'd better be out of it," said Katherine darkly. "He doesn't read poetry."

I repeated it was time he did—in a place like this. It would help him to "get away with it." (I could be slangy too.)

"The place doesn't give him any trouble—he stands it much better than we do. It makes us mildly insane."

"It does all that!—and yet I would not part with my insanity for the price of his content, if he is content. He oughtn't to be: he's got a soul."

"Have you asked him?" Katherine mocked.

"I don't say it has aches in it, but Tennyson will put some there; or define any special ache he may have developed since I talked with him last."

"Merciless woman! You are the most dangerous person to be with the young! Why do you want to drag him into our company of lunatics? We know what we are and we discount the fact when it's likely to interfere with the business of life. I do! Leave him alone."

"Well, it's done: I've sent for the books, but we needn't give them to him."

The books would come after she had left us; I reflected that I should need them if Kayding did not. I shall never be too old for "Locksley Hall" nor old enough for "Fifty Years After." And in those weeks I was growing more and more insane, as my daughter called it.

One day, to my amazement, I made her blush. I asked—point-blank: "What do you and Tony talk about?"

"He's a bully rider," she parried rather fiercely. "Talk is no good when you can ride. I shall never ride again, it's likely—" It was then she colored up.

Another day, a little later, her father broke out, gathering temper and turning red as she had. "How in thunder can she stand so much of him! What are you up to, Lucy?"

"I'm not doing anything."

"You started this riding game. Can't you see it's going too far?"

"I see nothing—I leave it to Katherine."

"You've baited your hook with a live man's—"

"He's only a boy!"

"Then can't you have a little mercy?

"Have mercy on me! The riding is our one chance."

"How much are you willing to stake on that chance?"

"Whatever may come of it—to him, poor dog. Fate will reward him."

"Suppose your fish runs away with the line, bait and all!"

"You're profane."

"Nothing is impossible in a place like this."

"There are times then when I could say—let it come if it will! We shall have had her a few years, in this place where 'nothing is impossible.' Those are the only places fit to live in."

"You are bewitched."

"I wish she could be. Can't you see? Katherine might be as happy as any woman ought to be in such a life as she could make of it here; it's not the place—nor for that matter the man. It's what such a woman as she is could put into them—him."

"Good God! I can believe that you love her, but that you value her!" He struck a match and another; his hand was unsteady—the matches went out. And he went out, my poor man. I followed and took his arm.

"Charley, I beg of you don't try to stop it now. She's perfectly sane if I am not."

"Why can't you leave her alone?"

"Does nature leave us alone? Spells are a part of nature when we're young."

"There's a difference in spells. If she is ours, she'll stay, anyhow; if something else calls her, she oughtn't to shirk. We've no right to lay traps—She came here to make us happy."

One night, the children, as unconsciously I often called them, were so late coming back to camp that I worried lest something might have happened to them; and was surprised when they did ride in, at the silence and the delay before Katherine reported herself as her custom was while Tony took the horses up the trail.

I went outside and listened; the horses were there at a little distance hanging their heads on each other's necks. Katherine and Tony were not in sight, nor did I hear voices. They were standing on the edge of the cliff close together face to face, both silent. Katherine had given him both her hands; he held them between his own, and looked long in her eyes before he kissed them and resigned them—no words. I slunk back just as Katherine passed our tent and paused, but did not enter. "Good-night, parents. Late, but all right. Good-night, mams; I'm going straight to bed. 'Scuse us for being so late." This was to me who had followed her, to signify that she did not care for our usual chat.

I grieved, lying long awake, over my poor Gareth, rustic knight of Arthur's court, brought face to face with the full light of his time, in a damsel like a flame; a beautiful beacon out of his reach, not safe to gaze

on too long, or one would turn away dazzled to the
dark. It was many a year since I had read "Gareth
and Lynette." I could read a fresh meaning in it, now.
Tony's Lynette would not mock him, neither would
she yield. No "morning star" would wake his soul to
bliss; no "star of eve" would prove his longing true.
Romance is never dead, but the romance of our time
has some odd phases of irony, and more than youthful
despair—aged despair over youth that will not gather
roses, but only wheat and corn. I tossed from one wish
to another; it would have cut me to pieces then if he
could have won her; yet how else should she make out
a life here with us whose life was done?

My good man's cot creaked once or twice in the
glimmering darkness. He, too, was feeling sorrow on
the air of night—coming down to us from that big
lonely house above where we had repaid kindness and
hospitality with desolation.

"What were they doing? They weren't riding all
this time!"

"She has given him his answer; she doesn't want to
talk of it, that's all."

"All!"

It was one of our still nights, the tide very low.
"Speak softly," said I.

"Well; you've had your Roman holiday. She was
happy enough; we might have done without the riding.
Do you call the 'experiment' a success?"

"It's no holiday for me. It's a crisis, a decision as
sharp as death."

"You mean that you could conceive of our giving him Katherine!"

"Please speak low! You and I will not have much to say about it, but if you corner me, I don't mind owning that I would give him Katherine, if that would keep her here. I think what ever she does now, after this, will go very far and part us very long. He has the same restfulness and sweetness and a sort of mystery, too, and the beauty and silence and melancholy that we love so on this shore. He's a shore-man." (Now that Tony was done for, I could see so much more in him than before.)

"He's all that," scoffed my husband, "and that's all he'll ever be. He'll stay on his shore and grow fast to it. He's doing, at his age, what I propose to do after forty-two years steady on the job, not counting preparation."

"What is he doing?"

"Just enough work to keep fit and not go into his funds too deep; for the rest, exactly what he likes. I don't know if he knows there is a war in Europe—"

"Happy man!"

"You can't talk to him on the same level."

"In some directions; not all, by any means. In some he's far above us."

"He isn't our kind of folks."

"Ah, there you are!" said I. "Suppose, for instance, he owned all this shore that you taunt him with because he only loves it, as we do; how would you feel then about a 'shore-man'? He has as much of a life as most young men can boast of who've only got money and land, and he has none of the vices too many of them have. All he lacks is the stimulus of a quicker, quickened, mind. He's asleep; the Sleeping Prince, instead of the Sleeping Beauty; and he *is* a beauty if you like."

"I don't like! You talk as if you were crazy."

"Anyhow, I want you to be just, to one of the sweetest souls I've ever—tampered with. Fate has reached him through us; we cannot throw him aside and say, 'not our kind'! If he isn't our kind, so much the worse for us. We're utter snobs not to see it."

"And you want Katherine to see it? Well, I say again, you may love her, but you can't admire her."

He gave me the last word: "Only a woman I do admire above all others could be trusted to marry a man like Tony and live with him here on this shore. And if things went wrong, I should say she had proved unworthy the gift of a heart like his to love her and such a pure start in character to shape to her hand."

He did not hear half of what I said, but he heard enough. The cot creaked his response.

After a while I got up courage to say to Katherine (this was when the rides had stopped suddenly and Tony came no more), "Why won't you tell me the whole story? I shall know it sooner or later." Tony would tell me—after she was gone.

"I don't want you to think he is sulking or anything; he's a good loser. I asked him not to come, forbade him, in fact. It was the least I could do."

A very poor least, I told her. "You might give him another chance. When a man knows he has spoken too soon, it tortures him not to let him retrieve himself."

"Are you such a daft woman as to think he's got a chance?"

"Well, then, tell me what to think!"

"I think we must cut this summer short. I meant to have stayed through September."

"Oh, child!" I groaned. (This was my "success!")

"It comes of selfishness. I don't want to go. I knew he was losing his head—so was I! But I thought, 'the man is speechless'; I'd let it go on till I'd had my visit with you. There are ways worse than words, though! You see, I've had no experience. Much as you admire me, it's a fact, mother, he's the first man who ever proposed to me."

"Because you wouldn't let them."

"Why did I let him! I was a fool. I saw the signs—I suppose I did; something was the matter. I knew the rides ought to stop. Oh, those evenings!" Katherine's hands unclasped from behind her head; she straightened up and frowned at me. "No more romance for this child!"

She spoke so naturally, I ventured to push her a little farther. "Men are never satisfied when they're shunted off in this way with a full head of steam on; it's cruel and it hurts too much. Give him a chance to recover his balance, anyhow—unless"—and now I went too far—"you are afraid of losing your own."

She dropped forward as if shot. I think she would have covered her face, but she was too proud. Exactly as she would have taken a mortal wound she took the self-accusing blush that submerged her, while she looked me in the eyes, her own hard and glittering with hot tears.

"You haven't much mercy on either of us, have you, mother?"

I thought of that night by the fire long ago when she asked me, seated on her father's knee, if I could forget her clothes even if she were dying. It was the same look. "While you are testing him, remember you may be testing me, too. What if I shouldn't stand the test? This place for you and me is like the spell that was flung around Cecy when you took her out of the desert and gave her San Francisco to play with. I have had my own deserts: this is the mirage that leads to death in a desert."

"Spare your mother, dear."

"Spare me, then."

She cast herself upon me, abolishing the physical distance between us.

"But he isn't a man you need be ashamed of loving," I almost whispered as we embraced.

"He's a man I would be ashamed to own I loved. If he were not beautiful to look at! We haven't a word to say to each other—do you know what that means? As for marrying him, I'd as soon he swam out to sea with me and we drowned out there together in the sunset."

I had struck the nerve that I had been feeling for. "But you will come back?" I persisted madly.

"Not if you live here."

"But now we are insane! This is all a dream."

"It's such an infernal dream that if I lived here I should end by marrying Tony."

"You might never wake up!"

"Oh, yes, I should. If I never did, that would be worse than all. Oh, mother, don't keep me; you will if you try hard enough. But you must not! You don't know what you do."

I watched them go up the hill, the beautiful, tragic young pair—on that last ride poor Tony, unconscious he was a parody, had begged of her. I thought what a comment on her "time" that a girl as poised as Katherine could say with such passion, such fear of being entrapped, such cold envisioning of consequences, that she would rather drown than share the life of that dear fellow at her side; my hurt, forgiving Tony! *I* could have loved him at her age—I loved him at mine. We don't often love those whom we have injured; but every hour since we had bruised him and thrown him aside (though this wasn't the way of it) his image had come back to me in speechless testimony of what he was in himself, all those qualities that were unmatched in my experience of young modern men. But modern girls, it seemed, did not want them, could not use them in their lives.

X

One week later; Katherine's first train-letter had come. I was writing to her, alone in camp once more, seated in front of the trunk-lid secretary. My effort was to be cheerful even to idiocy: I must not be a bad loser either.

I babbled of our camp doings that week. The men were catching fish at last—pompanos in shoals; so many they hadn't time to clean them.

"The scheme is to cut the thick meat from their little backbones and fry it in collops. Remember John Ridd and his 'collops' of venison? Or they make those collops into a fish-pie with a crust of cornmeal most delectable. Our little stove is doing marvels. They turned it up on its head the other day and drummed a lot of stuff out of its in'ards; it's been baking beautifully ever since. Last night the old Chinaman of Chinaman's Rock, the sea-moss gatherer, came down the shore-path, his baskets swinging, and stopped at the cook-tent to offer me, grinning like an old seal, a bag of candy he had walked to town to buy. 'My fliend,' as he calls daddy, had paid him fifty cents for digging a can of sand-fleas for bait—'Too much!—I go town buy candy; you eat em—sabe?' We are not only honest but proud! It was a trying moment for me as he waited to see me eat some of the candy on the spot; but our conversation about you helped me out. Where was 'girl'? he asked. We told him. 'She live New York? She got husband?' He found it quite impossible to grasp the fact of a husband-less daughter setting up for herself in New York with parents in California. I am sure he thinks you can't be respectable. So you see we are of one date and creed as to daughters, old Chin and I ... There's the car now, daddy's own particular slam. They went to town for bread and the newspaper...."

"Want to go to Sand Point?" Charley stood in the tent-door hauling the paper out of one pocket, a bunch of letters from the other which he sorted while I gathered my wishes on the question.

"I don't know that I care so much for Sand Point. If you'll drop me at *the* Point, and stop for me on your way back," I maundered.

"No; we'll let you walk home or you can stay there all night," said he, grinning.

I put away my letter and got into an old Burberry of many seasons which I like to fold about me when spending an afternoon on the shore. Bundled up in this way I used to sit beside Katherine—in a silk blouse, sweaterless often, and the wind blowing over her in a steady stream. And her cheeks deep rose! and her hand as warm as a school-boy's.

We no longer crawled under the wires at the Point; we had discovered there was a sort of gate, merely a section of the fence attached to a movable post which one was expected to put back and replace the loop of wire over its head; one of Mr. Morehouse's typical gates. We found it open. A big dark-blue car stood empty a little way farther in the field.

Charley remarked, "There are people in here."

I glanced at the car and said, "I don't mind that kind of people." He saw me into the field (I would not let them drive me in), and when we had fixed our place of meeting I went on alone. As I passed the blue car I read the initials on the door, "P. M. D." They meant nothing to me, and just then I was thinking, "If I owned a car like that I wouldn't wear a coat like *that*." It was a woman's coat but not a lady's, I had casually observed, though it might have been as expensive as the car proportionately. There were two persons at a distance seated out on the cliff; having located them I knew where to go myself.

The rocks down on my projecting ledge, which was the spot I sought, are thrown together in wild and almost theatrical grandeur in miniature; a dwarfed sublimity. We called it rather sentimentally "Norman's Woe." I crept down to my own place on a rock joined to the cliff from where I had often waited for my fisherman, seated on his own rock separated from mine by a deep gut between. The action of the waves in this chasm I had watched for hours, as the tide, compressed within its jaws by the force of the surf behind it, tore in and sucked out again with murderous power. The kelp-plants rooted on its sides bent shuddering, and their long tresses streamed on the outward wave like the hair of drowned women.... I was not long there alone. Voices were approaching, a man's voice and a woman's and they were quarreling coarsely. It struck me I had never heard such a wrangle in such abandoned tones except on the stage in roles intended to excite derision and disgust. I shrank back into my niche, determined to avoid them. The man said little, but his words were oaths. The woman began to sob hysterically. They were now on the other side of the rock above me; to have attempted to escape I should have found myself almost in their laps. And then I saw the man. He broke away from his companion and sprang past me, and as he turned I saw his face. It was my son-in-law, Peter Dalbert, ruddy and smart and handsome, but in what I should call a beastly, towering rage.

He thundered to the woman to stay back—she came straight on, following him, and I saw her too, but I hardly know how to describe her. There was a woman there somewhere in the likeness of a doll, life-size, dressed in what the shops call "sport-clothes," an old fat doll, old eyes in the painted, plastered face, old fat hips, and fat ankles laced into high boots with heels that were a peril at every step as she toddled along. Suddenly she saw me; our eyes met, and I realized she was not old; she could not have been older than Katherine. That was the horror of it, what those eyes had seen. There was nothing left in life for her to weep for, yet her powdered lids were swollen, her eyes swam because she had taken too much wine, as her gait showed and her wild, coarse babbling.

Peter had sprung onto the fishing-rock and he warned her back from the chasm; for a man the leap is nothing. It was madness for her, but she took it before our eyes—Peter and I, who had not seen each other, but were watching her. She landed on the rock by a miracle, was there for a breath and flung out her hands for help—involuntarily I sprang. I saw them both face to face, the sea awash around them; Peter jumped back. I could not possibly be mistaken: he shrank from her clutch and the impact of her body. The rock is slippery and there was danger both might have had to go. He saved himself and she reeled backward and went down. The floor of the gut is paved with pointed rocks as one may see at low tide and the force of the wave sucking out is death itself.

I can't recall what may have happened next; but Peter was beside me and we were staring one at the other.

"Did you see that?" he choked. I nodded. "There was no room. I stepped back to give her room."

"You stepped back to save yourself. All she needed was a hand."

"You're mistaken," he chattered. "I saw I couldn't stop her and I gave her room."

"There was room. She reached out and you weren't there. You saved yourself."

"I won't say you lie, but what you said just now is a lie, a damned lie."

"It doesn't matter. Go away!"

"What doesn't matter!" he shouted at me like a man insane. "You've got to get this straight before we leave the place."

"It doesn't matter that a woman like that has lost her life. And it doesn't matter that I know you are a coward; I've always known it. Go away. I never want to see you again."

"I'll get a boat," said he, wretchedly rambling on.

"What will you do with it? A boat couldn't live a minute out there."

"I'll get a launch and come in from outside. She could swim."

"She could! You know as well as I do that no one will ever see her again. But you will see me—we shall see each other, for years! Don't forget what I have seen."

When he left the Point or where he went I cannot say. I crept away that I might not see or hear him. But it was some time before I gathered strength to climb the rocks, and there was not sun enough on the cliff to warm me. I crowded myself into such a hollow lined with mesembryanthemum as Katherine and I had found—the smell of the dead summer's flowers made me weep for our last talk there, she with her cheek against mine; and I felt like saying, O God! when I thought of Cecily. Had she ever driven beside Peter

in that car? It could not be an hour since I strolled
through the pasture and read the letters on the door....

I decided to walk to Sand Point and gave it up
feeling too weak, and dreading the highroad. Any one
meeting me I thought must see what I had seen in my
face, my eyes. I must avoid Peter too. It would be better
in every way to wait. What would he do with that
woman's coat? Burn it or steal down to the sea in some
safe place and throw it in? He would report nothing
that had happened while I lived. There was a ghost at
that spot for him and me. He and I to go linked forever
by this ghastly secret! And I had thought it something
to bear when we gave up Katherine to the higher life
she had chosen!

All our exquisite summer smeared with this
loathsomeness. Its gray days of covered lights and
low-hanging mist on the moorlands and monster
seas rolling in from nowhere; its days when we woke
to a cloudless sky, hot sun on the tent and a wine-
dark sea; its days of accentuating blackness with a
battering north wind, when the shore defied us to
stay, threw dust on us and tore at our tent-ropes and
slatted every-thing about our ears;—all our walks and
talks on the shore-path and evenings by the fire, the
dreams tinged with hovering sadness, the hopes that
were untenable, our fairy moonlights and raptures and
repressed desires. I speak in terms of youth as well as
age, my age and those young things whose troubles
were as my own: all smudged out in one blot of shame
and ugly horror. No lyric lights and shadows, none

of nature's half-tones; nothing on my old gray rocks
to see now but a woman's crazed colors, a woman
shrieking like a mænad, and a man—my daughter's
husband—telling me a lie—a coward's lie, to hide his
unspeakable infamy. The father of our grandchildren!
I could not possibly share this with my husband; he
would see red.

I suppose we did not look at each other much out-
of-doors; we knew each other's battered visages pretty
well by this time and there were always the horizon and
the sea and the beloved old fields beyond us. We were
halfway home when Charley turned to me and said (it
was then I decided I could never tell him): "Did you
have a good time at the Point? You ought to have come
with us. You look cold."

"I am cold," said I.

"You've caught cold! Take some aspirin as soon as
we get back."

I said it over, settling it with myself: If I must
be dragged to the Point to keep tryst with Peter and
his unclean ghost, I would keep that tryst alone. The
horror should not spread. And I had a woman's dread
withal of a man's heavy hand, his downright fist in an
affair of such complexity that my own brain reeled with
it. I felt like one who carries a brand of fire through a
room all draughts and delicate draperies ready to catch
a spark. Let no one spring to help me; I must not be
spoken to nor jarred.

We had tied up the tent on leaving it, and our
little snuggery seemed close to us on our return.

Charley opened up everything, but soon I was shivering with cold. He ordered me to take my dose at once. I went mechanically to the trunk (which has drawers and stands on legs when it is in domestic use) for the aspirin; there lay my letter to Katherine. It would never be finished; I laid it away with the date, thinking—"The last day, if I had but known it, when we could have said, 'How happy we are!'"

I try to see myself as I was then, a woman of the past. What I am now or am likely to be, I do not say: the present is too strange, the future too unguessable. But at that time I was one of the women who say they "don't believe in divorce" as positively as one would say it of suicide. There is Quaker blood in our family; not close, but it is a tenacious influence. The Quaker divorce is limited to separation, and of course there is no remarrying among them. Much suffering is the result in special cases, and the principle involved in bearing it does not comfort much the individual sufferer; nor did it comfort me when I thought of my own daughter. But I should have clung to my Erasmian belief that the evils of the bond must be cured within the bond. Cecy, at her age, not wise, and very beautiful, would be almost sure to remarry (in the case of a divorce, loving the second man no more, perhaps, than she had loved Peter)—this I faced also. In regard to Peter I should have to go on with my Victorian hypocrisies in public, but when he and I were alone with our ghost, I should be the unsleeping moment which had revealed him to himself before a witness who would never forget; who would not scold and forgive him as had been done hundreds of times. I loved him no more than nature loves us. I would be memory that neither accuses nor forgives—merely restates a fact ineffaceably on record.

XI

From Peter to Tony! Peter as I saw him, always scorching away in the big blue car with that woman's coat beside him. The car was like his life, polished outside, strong and mechanically perfect, the costliest thing on the market, adapted to speed and pleasure, but not choice in what it carried. Tony I saw as he used to ride up the lonely moor-road beside Katherine. His horse was any horse, the rider was at home, one of nature's perfect adjustments; there was rhythm in every line of his body, and I knew his soul on those evenings was like the lark at heaven's gate. These accidental wild fancies came at any time—when Tony was beside me, perhaps, not rhythmical at all, quite dumb, tramping through the weeds to leave me the whole path. I hardly know what I should have done without him in those dark days; he was the mainstay of my faith in young manhood in a world that looked so vile. I saw that he was proud of his sorrow, as those who are humble can well be.

"You mustn't mind that I know all about it," I had said to him. It was on the first evening after Katherine left us; he had seen me walking the shore-path alone and came down and walked beside me. "I love you for loving her. And now, will you forgive me? It was I who planned the riding—urged it; it was a piece of abominable selfishness."

"But that is all I have! What could you have done for me more than those rides? I shall thank you all my life."

"Oh, Tony, you will do a great deal with your life. You have only to be patient." I should not have said "be patient"; it might mislead.

"Will there ever be any more summers like this?" he asked, rending my heart.

"Never, I think, like this. But we had our chance—we've both failed; and yet we have not failed quite if we can say we did not spoil our chance. You, I am sure, can say so. You are a proud loser."

"Yes, I had my chance; I thank Doctor Benedict for that. I owe it to him that I was free."

Could he tell me what that meant, I asked, and repeated his last word.

"That I wasn't married," he answered bluntly. "I was free to do my best."

"But, do you thank your friend for that?"

"I should like to tell you why I do, if I could tell it right. You might think it strange. But he was not eccentric; and he had the same right to ask it that a father might have."

"Do tell me. Nothing in this world is strange!"

"He wanted me to be a doctor and take his practice after him. It wasn't my choice, but I had no real choice then. He saw the boys and girls around here marrying as soon as they grew up; he wanted me to study and work at a profession till I was well on to thirty—as I am now, without the profession. I was only fourteen when he asked me if I could promise him to leave the girls alone—not to think of marrying any girl till my work was done. It didn't seem much of a promise then. But after a while it got hard." (The girls may have made it harder, I fancied; he must have been a young Hylas in his adolescence.) "I was so afraid I might be a fool before I could catch myself that I kept away from the young people here in town. It was a good thing in some ways, in some ways not; I am a stupid fellow in company. But that is probably the reason, seeing that I was a fool, why I didn't do like the others."

"I don't know that you were a fool." I asked this to test him. "It might have been better—you'd have escaped this summer planted in the midst of your life, which comes to nothing. Do I taunt you? I want you to face the thing. Though I shouldn't have known, or dreamed that you had had your struggle."

"It wasn't a struggle—that!" said Tony hotly. "I've told it wrong. I was a boy. I am thankful to God now, that I was free. If I had been married when I met her, I shouldn't have dared to look at her again."

"But you mustn't waste your life on a dream. You haven't asked, but I must tell you, there is scarcely a hope. She did her best for us both. If we couldn't keep her, if she could not stay for us, she never would for you unless she cared almost to madness. And you know her! She is too 'sadly wise'—She loves all this too well! She tears herself away from it as from an enchantment." Here I was, trying to detach him, yet insanely giving him hope. Or was he too modest to see it?

"What you have to bear I can bear," said he. "There is only one thing that would hurt more than I could stand and stay here and wait—"

"I didn't say 'wait' for her, Tony, my dear boy—don't misunderstand me!"

His chest heaved. "I have no right to ask;—is there another man?"

"There is no other man, and yet I should not call her free."

I tried to explain to this shore-man how my daughter lived in New York, sharing a little flat with another girl who paid her half of their modest expenses out of her earnings and helped support a mother; a splendid, uncompromising girl whom I admired and feared. Those were the sort of influences that governed her life now. She called herself a slacker loafing out here, playing with her old parents on their shore.

He listened, absorbed, and asked for more details about her work. I gave them with as much conviction

as I could command: the Wiser Mothers and Better
Babies that were the aim and problem of these maiden
mothers who were giving away their youth. We were
cold and heart-sick, both of us, each selfish as nature is,
each thinking our selfishness the appointed salvation
of that youth which tore itself out of the clutch of
nature's spells. But for him it was worse than for me; it
was wrecking his simple life and all the satisfactions it
might have held. Once more I pressed him: could he
be glad of the summer that was past—knowing there
might never be another?

"Always," said he, as if he swore it. "Why not
Better Men? That she has done for me. Only, I ask you
to let me know if there ever is another man." His face
flushed darkly.

"I promise you I will," said I. "And now I will give
you your Tennyson."

His eyes questioned me as to the "now," but he
asked no answer. Nor did he seem, I am bound to say,
very thrilled by the prospect of my gift.

I asked him another home-question: why had his
studies stopped?

"Because he died."

"Doctor Benedict?"

"It was his ambition, not mine. But I ought
not—well, I broke down, in the will to work, that's the
truth of it. Poor Aunt Luisa saw it; *she* has ambition.
I did go up to Berkeley to take my examinations,
but it was soon after his death. The crowds on the
campus bothered me—but it was just as bad after I

got home…. This winter I am going to work. I'm not going to be caught that way again."

"What way, Tony?"

"Oh, in the backwash of things that can't be helped. Will poetry be the best thing to read?"

"It won't be the only thing. You must ask my husband for some of the big 'he books,' as he calls them. I give you what *I* love, but that is not enough."

Another day I asked him why he did not work up his examinations again and take the U.C. course even now. He answered nervously, "I'm too old. I couldn't stand those boys and girls." The "supremely afflicted," as has been written, can only be helped in their own way.

XII

My camp-mate was growing restless. He must
have seen that I had given up the Point, and I
hoped he might have connected the fact with our
disappointment about Katherine; he did not allude to
that, which was like him. He only asked if I had lost all
interest in the place, if it didn't "wear well."

"I've lost interest in everything, and so have you!"
Suddenly I broke down. "Let us go East. We need
some real talk. We are too far away from everything
here—it will drive us mad." He looked at me gravely;
I don't think he was surprised. "You have got to go to
Washington. Leave me in New York with Katherine. I
don't want to be gay; we are sure to be in Washington.
I should have to get clothes."… And the next day, after
this break in our silence, we were motoring up to Half-
Moon Bay where Cecily was sending a car to meet me,
he to go back alone.

A telegram had been forwarded with our mail, from the nurse who was with her, saying that Mrs. Dalbert was ill. Would like me to come up. "Nothing serious," the message added, "but confined to her bed." At last accounts Cecily had been at Tahoe and I was wondering if Peter had gone up there, and wondering about other things that in happier circumstances are none of a mother's business. Also I had been watching our daily paper for news of any "Disappearance" that would correspond to that scene I had witnessed. Even without the name, circumstances might have pointed to Peter's companion; but no hint of any such tragedy had found its way into print: from the gulf she had come, to the gulf she had returned. When this news arrived of Cecily's sudden illness I could but connect the fact with some mental shock, since no accident was mentioned. There were other papers that we did not see, and there was Peter, that incalculable fool.

But my first words with the nurse as she took me up to Cecily's room explained her illness. It was from most "natural causes"; the unnatural confusion and despair it wrought in a mother's mind I need not describe. During our winter visit with Cecily I had not been blind to the attitude between her and Peter; no confidences passed her lips, but I had concluded there would be no more children. The situation must have changed even since Katherine's visit. Cecily grieved over her disappointment; this I could understand as a fact apart from causes and contingencies; but I saw she was wistful and tender in those directions, too,

and my wretched heart stood still. What was to be the
future of this marriage where the persistence, in spite
of everything, of love on the young wife's part, filled
her own mother with shame and actual horror? Peter
was not made of deceit; he could lie, but he was not a
deliberate, living lie in his life that I was aware of; nor
was he, as I in my haste had called him, an incalculable
fool. One could calculate that he would be one
frequently, but he was not consistently a fool either.
He was insensible. His satisfaction with himself under
all circumstances was the one thing to count on; he
had never in his own eyes been to blame for anything.
It was a moral lacquer as finished as the varnish on his
cars. Loving himself as he did, how could he be wrong!
This in effect and for a measurable length of time
might deceive a girl no cleverer than Cecy.

He was at this time "on the water wagon," as it
is merrily called by those who on occasions join the
ride. If he had not looked so fit and gay, I might have
taken it to mean precaution on his part, recollecting
the old adage about wine and truth. But he seemed to
remember nothing, except to keep out of my way. In
no respect was he quelled or dogged by what should
have been his nightmare clutching him by the hair.

When I go back to the state of mind I was in
throughout that impossible visit, I lose the power
to think clearly, to define its situations, its torturing
demands. I saw my child's recovered hopes, her
sprightliness and her pride in her husband's attentions
so long lacking. He was her devoted lover; he filled her

room with flowers; there were other flowers, but his she gave the place of honor, displaying them to me, wore them and kept them by her bed. Her pillows were scented with his cigars; a certain chair was always at the bedside, his chair (which I also occupied). I heard their voices and laughter in my own room adjoining, where I retired when his step came flying up the stairs. She was meeting him more than halfway. She would ask me if I had seen him yet? He was looking so well! And why did I always leave the room when he came up to see her?

"He's not a shy boy," she hinted. "He's very sweet to me these days. He wanted this baby!" The exclamation-point is mine, to mark why I rose and left the room.

I took my breakfast in bed, though I hate the custom. At luncheon Peter was never in and Cecily's not coming down made an excuse for his never dining at home. Thus I had been in the house nearly a week before we encountered each other. But one evening he gave me his company at dinner. When dessert came on the table I rose; but he followed me almost immediately into the library, where usually I sat awhile and read the evening papers. And there we had this extraordinary conversation.

He began with my name: "Mrs. Cope" (he had never addressed me except in this formal manner), while we are here by ourselves, will you let me say something? When Cecy was taken ill, you know, I thought you might have written—that you must have told her. I was all off. I want to thank you."

I did not believe for a moment that he wanted to thank me; he merely wished to sound me on the question whether I intended to speak later, when Cecily might be better able to bear my communication. And I answered him accordingly:

"Peter, I have always thought you had a very common mind."

It took him half a minute to get around this not over-subtle speech. Having grasped it, he remarked sullenly: "You think I'm pretty common, anyhow, but I hand it to you on this! I don't know another woman, not one, who wouldn't have spoken." I kept silence. After fidgeting a little, he asked with a certain diffidence, "But you have told the General?"

I said he forced me to repeat myself; and that made him angry, and he said, "Why do you give me this rough stuff, when all I meant was to show I can appreciate a little consideration?"

"For you?"

He swallowed the emphasis, flushing. "Don't you ever intend to say anything?"

"Not unless I lose my mind."

This was all he wanted; he could defy me now with a fine show of recklessness: "I wish you would speak to the General—get it off your system. He may not see it just as you do. And you didn't see it as it was." He eyed me hardily.

I rose to leave the room.

From habit he started to open the door, when I paused to say: "My husband knows a great many vile things that he spares me. I shall spare him this—for the present."

Raging, he sat down again, and I went out and shut the door for myself.

But revenge was easy. He was getting it day by day and being paid for it. Peter, I have no doubt, could make love to a lady as correctly as he could take wine with a gentleman; that side of his education had been attended to. Both exhilarants might stop within bounds or be carried to the point of intoxication. He had passed that point in remaking love to his wife and was proud of it—he welcomed the old spell. It helped to lay ghosts. And she, in her restored confidence, was touched and grateful. She was infused with the joy of his strong young presence, flushed with love and welcoming her love. It contributed to her recovery. The nurse, who admired Peter, said sympathetically, "They are like a new-married pair." I saw nothing of what passed between them; I saw its effects; the growing shyness in her eyes, her dreadful little coquetries of dress in preparation for his visits. He sent her beautiful new clothes to try on; he bought her splendid jewels. At last she was pronounced well enough to drive out with him. He carried her downstairs (she was perfectly able to walk), exquisitely dressed, radiant as a rose. It was so I encountered them—I saw her cling with her arms around his neck and the long kiss he gave her on her lips. And he put her in the blue car—! Did I wish him dead? I could not have assisted his death, but I

wondered what could be done with his life. I continued
to see him in the light of my own punishment and
myself as his. We were fated to work out the sum
between us. But I had no plan; none of my theories of
marriage or divorce fitted this case (perhaps because
it was the case of my own daughter), only my instinct
was to stop this infatuation on her part. It is impossible
not to feel that vice embraced must communicate its
stain.

I have no idea that he was defying me or that he
had any thought at all except pride in being not quite
so often intoxicated in one way and more so in another
sweeter and fresher way, and equally at his demand. He
had no more spiritual imagination than a well-bred dog
of a fashionable breed. He was shameless, but I think it
was because he was so limited.

My dear man wrote that he intended to break
camp that day week. He had reached a pitch of
boredom that had driven him up on the hill evenings
to talk with Kayding.

"He's a queer Dick. He has got a collection of
quite hard facts under those movie-star curls. We
talked about land and crops and irrigation; he's better
posted agriculturally than on flocks and herds. I asked
him about goats; there's a market for goats' milk away
beyond supply. Goats can live anywhere—" I found
myself really unable to finish about these goats; it made
me feel wild. But I longed for the atmosphere this letter
came out of as a gasping prisoner longs for the sky.

My visit now was soon to close. I waylaid Peter the next morning, leaving my room as I heard him leave Cecily's; we met at the stair-head. I asked for a few minutes alone with him that evening. Cecy was coming down to dinner for the first time, but she would go up early. "I won't detain you long," I said.

"Certainly—as long as you please," he added airily, as he waited for me to precede him down the stairs. His politeness had a tinge of sarcasm.

Cecily was in high color and spirits that evening after a second longer ride. She wore a new evening dress and asked my opinion of the shade of pink, which struck me as immoral somehow, an unnatural pink. I said I did not care for those made-pinks.

"But all pinks are made," said Cecy, seriously defending Peter's taste.

"Not this pink," said he, touching her cheek softly with the back of one finger.

… Anger is my note of failure; the climbing wretchedness and disgust in my heart had reached the point where I found it difficult to control my voice, which is, of course, a fatal way to begin a lecture supposed to proceed from a higher plane than that of the person lectured.

"Peter," said I when we were alone, "you must not think you can play with my silence. We are not confederates. The secret between us *I* hold over *you*; I reserve the power to speak if ever it shall be necessary. It will be, when I am convinced that you are without shame or the possibility of remorse. I thought so yesterday afternoon."

"Yesterday afternoon," he repeated, growing slowly heated and lowering his eyes. "Where did I see you yesterday afternoon?"

"You didn't see me; I saw you—on the stairs, with Cecy in your arms. You put her in that car—"

"Well; what do you propose to do about it? It was my wife and my car."

"There is a law to protect wives and children from husbands like you—when there is no law of decency in the man himself. You have no more right to kiss Cecy than I have to tell you so. We are on common ground, and I have no more respect for your rights as a husband than you have shown for hers as a wife. Take yourself in hand and I will be silent; but if you go on in this shameless self-indulgence, self-satisfaction, I will show you up as you are: the most contemptible object in the shape of a man that I have ever seen in my life."

"For the gracious God! Who made you my judge?"

"I am not your judge, but I am your wife's mother. Why I should have been called to be that woman's witness there at the Point, God, as you say, may know. But I am her witness. Don't take what you have no longer any right to and smirk about it and play the loving husband right before my eyes. You are a lost man as she was a lost woman, but she paid her price in full, and you nothing. And are taking more!"

"Do you want me to go and kill myself now because I didn't do it at the Point?"

"*I* want! What does the law say? Human law, which is supposed to take the place of conscience? Have you ever had a conscience, Peter? Dig it up and be that law to yourself."

"Are you talking about divorce?"

"Divorce punishes both, and *you* are the sinner. Punish yourself. You know what you have forfeited—give Cecy the freedom of her person as the law would give it."

"She doesn't want it."

"She must have it, or she shall be told why she has to have it. Do you understand me?"

"I understand a threat," said he. "You threaten me with a divorce cooked up by yourself."

"Nothing of the kind. I demand from you some test of character; if you love your wife, are you not able to protect her from yourself until you become something less vile, and *be* it?"

Peter looked at me with a crimson face. "I see; I'm on probation—Well, I'll go away. I see what you want: grounds for a divorce without any scandal. Perhaps I can accommodate you. Do you think Cecy will thank you?"

"You are purposely trying to misunderstand me. I haven't asked you to leave your wife; that isn't paying the price yourself for being untrue to her. That is desertion."

"Well, I say! I don't see myself sitting around here handing tea. I'm her husband or I'm not. Take your choice. If you want to threaten me, start that lie about what you saw! It's your word against mine. What you want is to cow me, see me blubbing on my knees. Not a hope! I'm off—I'd go to hell tonight if I was sure I'd never see you again."

He sat on one side of the fire digging at the coals, I on the other shivering and sick with a feeling of impotence. Neither of us had raised our voices during this terrific and ridiculous scene. Two persons, as different as we were, locked in a word-combat could not but be absurd,—like deaf and dumb people quarreling. The nurse's low, pleasant voice asked, as she opened the door after a slight knock which we did not hear, if Mr. Dalbert would be coming up again—Mrs. Dalbert wanted to know. If not, she would get her patient ready for bed.

Peter sprang up and turned his back immediately to the speaker. "Eh?—Oh, no. Tell her I'm going out. Sorry." The door closed again, and we heard the nurse go down the hall for her bedtime tray.

"You tell Cecy anything you like, Mrs. Cope. You've got me buffaloed. Now run the show yourself. I shan't hinder you."

"If you are going away, Peter, that is only more cowardice in my opinion."

"I've had enough of your opinion. I'm only a man with a 'common mind.' If it's separation you want, we'll separate on the common plan. No fancy living together and not living together. Tell Cecy it's your doing."

Peter went to Tahoe the next day to fetch home
the little boys, he said. They had been left at the Inn
with their nurse and grandmother when Cecy's illness
came on and she was hurried down to the city. On the
following day they arrived with their nurse alone; Peter
had remained at the Inn. His mother was there, but
Cecy, I am sure did not believe that had been his reason
for staying. So far as I knew he had sent her no word.
She could not hide her intense chagrin. It was the old
Peter, irresponsible, oblivious of others, and faithless to
any resolve, absorbed from day to day in the pursuit of
his own wishes.

It was only the old mother she said goodbye to
on the day after this fresh blow. I had not expected
her to be much moved by my going, though our visit
had been especially dear and comforting as between
our two selves: mothers will "keep." But *I* was moved.
With me there was a revival of all the old pangs
that had slept a little in the past few years of vague
uneasiness in regard to Cecily. It had been more than a
distance of miles that parted our lives. But now I was
in the very heart of her troubles, unknown to her. I
had taken Peter in hand, or he had been, as I felt and
feared, thrust into my hands, and I was not holding
him; and still I might be accountable for whatever
inconceivable turn he should take as a consequence
of my interference. Yet I could not speak; there was
nothing for me to say, unless I told all.

With this hidden knowledge I left my child,
regretting now the decision to go East. I went on

with it, however. I went over to Berkeley and opened our little house and got in a cleaning woman and mechanically did all that a house-keeper has to do in preparation for sub-letting even such a small place as that, for we had been lucky enough to find a tenant. Her father drove up from camp and spent one night with Cecily; our camp-stuff, the car and trailer, he stored with Harvey's help in her big garage. He shook hands with Harvey for us both, and we packed and went East. Of all that followed—Cecily's long trial as it proved to be—month after month, filled with a thousand rumors and speculations which she could not put into letters, I knew only through those letters. They were full of a proud wife's determined effort to hide her humiliation, and for that I respected my poor girl, but it was sickening not to know more, not to be able to tell her what I knew.

From Tahoe Peter had wired her that he was going to New York to say good-bye to an old classmate who was off for France. Peter had never put himself out to observe such ceremonies, his friendships did not hamper his plans; she put no faith in this excuse, but it was all he ever gave. After that she heard no more. The line was cut between them by his own act and desire apparently. She learned from the friend weeks later that Peter was not with him; they had gone across together, but Peter had remained in London—what to do there he had not said. His mother appeared to know no more than his wife, though she had seen him last. His business communications were through a bank in

London which guarded his address as if it were a club; at his request undoubtedly. He had, in the current speech, submerged.

I can give only the bare facts, which sound incredible. Charley shrugged his shoulders and said not a word. Cecy must have had suspicions that she did not impart to me with regard to Peter; of his mother she said once that her silence was not a "sympathetic silence," that she was unable to "get at her. She thinks, of course, that I must be to blame." My own silence might have been called traitorous, yet *I* did not speak; nor could I, under the circumstances, blame Madam Dalbert. She was as proud as Cecily; and her silence, like my own, might be touched with remorse. Peter was not dead, of course, while he could be in receipt of remittances; and he was not lost. London did not care where he was, nor the world—nor even his own little world of San Francisco's gay set. He was not an important part of any world. I seemed to be involved in the old fatality, testing those I loved best. Here was Cecy's ordeal—at my hands! The test of her love and the sifting of *her* character. We had never thought, her father and I, that she was greatly endowed with "character"; now we should see.

XIII

What a winter it was, that first winter of our neutrality! We stepped into the waves of war-talk off our shore, as it were, with gasps of excitement, saying to each other, "How much closer it seems"; and still it was only the ground-swell. New words rushed into our daily speech, the war slang that had not reached us in the West. We met old friends, whose opinions we had taken for granted were the same as our own in all fundamental ways, and found ourselves estranged; for we had not lost faith in argument, and no one could let the war alone. They talked in Boston and we talked in New York, and what they were saying and doing in Washington we did not know, but we had the darkest suspicions. Gossip came to us in letters from old army chums, guarded to a degree, and from friends of the former administrations, not guarded at all; every one seemed to feel bitterly that in Washington this was not considered "our war."

Katherine was an absorbed reader, but not one of the eager talkers; she listened to all of us and gibed at our readiness to misunderstand one another's heated words when we practically meant the same thing. She worked hard at her "job" and showed no excitement; one never can tell, though, with those who consume their own smoke. As I walked at her side I thought her adorable in her dark, slim street-clothes and little black hat that hid her hair. Her cheek in the cold was a deeper rose, but its outline looked a trifle wan; she was certainly thinner and too white around the mouth; when I spoke of it anxiously she only laughed.

The first thrill of our reunion passed and we settled into our winter schedule. We lived at a little hotel across the square from her apartment and dined in its café when we had to. It was an old beloved neighborhood with many associations for us, and old friends cropped up every day; hers were all new. The girl I have spoken of as dreading, who shared her housekeeping and kept their mutual accounts and paid the bills in manly fashion, called Katherine her "wife." (This struck us as "new.") All the girls, the sturdy workers or the mere charmers lapped in luxury, with consciences burdened by wealth, like our dear, brilliant Helen, one and all made up to my old general and spoiled him as if old men had no vanity. Between husband and daughter (every one seemed to love

Katherine) I went about in a reflected glory trailing clouds of borrowed admiration.

Our poor rustic knight never entered our talks, nor our minds, I fear, speaking for my own. Katherine's mind was more or less a mystery to the mother who bore her. When I thought of Tony, he was all one with what I imagined the camp to be in winter:

"Oh, the dreary, dreary moorland,
Oh, the barren, barren shore!"

Dun colors on the moorlike fields, high surfs and deep-toned sunsets, cakes of ashes and pebble-floors open to the rain where our tents had stood, and when the early night came down no lights along the shore but Pigeon Point, and Tony's lamp where he sat alone in one corner of the great empty house of winds and squeaking rats "poring over miserable books." Or did he, like other rustics, like the watchman and his wife, go to bed and to sleep what time we should be rising from our dinners!

Katherine called me that winter, observing her mother from a new angle, the most impressionable person of my "age" she had ever known; I wondered if this had anything to do with Tony? I threw things off, she said, and took things on like a girl of sixteen. To a certain extent I dare say she was right; but it was such a winter! My hideous talks with Peter, the scenes he had fastened on my memory, all were as true admittedly and as unbelievable as the things we were hearing about in Belgium and France. Whenever I read one of Cecily's proud, disturbed letters I felt like a criminal, almost as if I had murdered Peter (having wished him dead). But the times were too great; the excitement of this intenser living to which we had long been strangers took possession of me and drowned the summer's past. And Tony went with it back into the vistas of dreamland; he might indeed have been a poor country squire or just-made knight of Arthur's court. Or he might have been a love-sick youth shut up in Locksley Hall. Though I never fancied him as morbid, sick in any sense.

I did go to Washington, after all—Charley over-persuaded me. I snatched up what Katherine called "a clo' or two" in the course of a morning's shopping (throwing away the economies of years) and we had one of the gay weeks that occasionally burst into our lives, regardless of expense. She welcomed the returned prodigal with a "tea"—to show off my new clothes, she mocked me. She had absolutely refused the afternoon gown we had wanted to give her. "I have no afternoons," she said. Indeed, most of the girls at the tea were in severest street-clothes. In "my time" we made ourselves pretty for a tea.

After they were gone, Katherine and I had the best of the occasion alone in the fire-lit dusk, the disjected remnants of the feast ungathered and the pantry dark. Katherine's "husband" had gone up town to some festivity of her own for the evening, mine was dining at his club to talk farming with an expert from the West—goats, perhaps.

"Didn't I *tell* you?" said Katherine.

"Tell me what?"

"That it would pass like a dream? It's a different element."

I knew what she meant, but I took up the gauge, as we always did when an old argument came up again. "We are not fishes nor fowls that we can't live but in one element."

She took a long, soft breath: "It's beauty—to break your heart, but it's death."

"Not at sixty."

"At twenty-six it is—or ought to be."

"Then why are there Idylls like Gareth and Lynette? Why do we want a 'hope' like that to come true?"

"Oh, you old Tennysonian! Idylls is idylls; and we are such children about our 'hopes.' We can't bear anything to end in pain. We can't stand truth. It's like dreaming you jumped off the house-roof and found you could fly. You don't try those things if you're awake; even if you're not awake, the result is the same."

"It seems to me in these times we can do anything."

"Except go back to our old dreams. It isn't as if the world were not full of dreams; why stick to that one kind? I'm only talking to myself, you know" (I was glad to know it)—"licking myself into shape. Let any one go in for personal happiness who can stand it; it would go to my head."

"It costs to be so wise—at twenty-six!"

"Last summer I was desperate. Thank Heaven, it was a dream! A good one if life were an idyll, but even you must confess its conditions might be wearing in time."

"Wisdom is said to be a trifle wearing; I speak from hearsay."

We smiled at each other sarcastically. She went down on the rug at my feet in one of her swift revulsions, fearing she had hurt me; she crossed her arms on my lap, looking up into my face, her own in shadow.

"The wisdom of daughters is wearing on mothers;—but, oh, mamsy, mamsy, what would you have done!"

"Well, it *is* done," said I, shrinking from my own recklessness. "Done, and done with! I admit we were insane."

"I have a queer feeling that nothing is ever done with. Do you never think of Tony? I've been thinking of him lately in the oddest way—waking up suddenly as if I had dreamed of him, which I never do, nor think of him much. But he's liable to come back on me in that fashion lately. I don't like it, but I don't consider it's my affair. Our sleep at least ought be to a 'forgetting.'"

She sat back and turned her profile to the firelight as if it were painted on gold.

"It's no wonder," said I, "that you don't know what to make of your parents, you young things; you think and speculate too much. You can't leave anything alone.

We army fossils know that we're an anachronism, but what are you going to do without us, just now? We're like my old Tennyson compared to your anarchists in verse—that isn't even prose!" (We had had many a "gay bout" on this theme.) "Think of us in the Philippines, three years! and you in Europe and England and New York!"

"Be patient, old dears. You and the crusaders are coming to your own! But that isn't what I want to talk about either. Long ago—do you mind if I smoke? I wrenched all your plans to pieces and took my own way. You've heard and you've seen now what we're up to. If one woman in the course of her working life could help, say, one hundred other women to feed their babies better, so half of them wouldn't die and the other half grow up deficient in some way—there you'd have an average of three or four hundred better Americans to three or four the one woman might produce if she went in for babies of her own. Isn't it good economics?"

"It depends on what is meant by 'better' Americans. The first woman's children might have turned out remarkable men, or a choice kind of woman, if she hadn't joined the third sex and refused to have any. Environment and teaching can't take the place of blood."

"Dear soul! That argument chases its own tail; you go round and round. And it's old as the flood. And your gibe about the third sex doesn't touch me, on your own showing. Doesn't blood teach us whom *not* to marry?"

She had touched the nerve in me. We both thought of Cecy. "Oh, mams, we must stop! Why do I hurt you? Because I love you and can't leave you alone. I want your approval! ... Little tormented mother. Can't you tell me—is there nothing you can say about Peter?"

"Nothing," said I. "You have read Cecy's letters; I can't even tell you anything about her."

Among my own old girlhood's friends who cropped up was one who lived in Boston. I paid her a visit of a week. While there Charley dutiously wrote to me, and in his last note he enclosed a letter which contained a very curious piece of news, Vallevista news. It was from Mr. Hoadley of mercantile memory and had the very flavor of a morning's gossip, as if we were seated on his store-bench.

He had but a thin excuse for writing, but his news poured out of him. Mr. Morehouse had died suddenly and left a will executed immediately after the suit brought by his nephews had been decided in his favor. He had not lost a day in "getting back at them," as Mr. Hoadley put it. The will was a very able document. Several rather powerful interests had been enlisted, through moderate legacies, in seeing that it was not broken. Ten thousand to the Sister's Orphanage ("he never took no notice of them before"), ten to the Presbyterian Church ("he ain't been inside it since I can remember"), five thousand to start a free circulating library in Vallevista ("that won't go far, and he don't own a book, I bet, but his account-books unless it was give to him")—thus Mr. Hoadley's comments ran. The nephews were left one dollar apiece and the remainder of the estate, all the lands and titles he was seized of, to Kayding—Tony—the witness to whom, as the testator no doubt had believed, he owed the vindication of his mental powers and the freedom of his last days.

"Everybody knows that trial took years out of him," Mr. Hoadley wound up; "it filled him up with bile. He died of it, you might say. For once the law done justice and everybody's glad to see it. Nobody wants them yellow dogs to get the land. They bit the hand that fed them. Tony don't seem excited about it. I asked him if he'd written to you. He said he hadn't. Wouldn't that jar you! After you 'most lived together down on the shore! So I thought I might as well write and tell you myself. It's the queerest thing that's happened here in fifty years, I might say a hundred. I want to say, too, every one knows Tony never so much as squinted at the idea of any price but his witness fees. But he don't say a word. I expect he's kind of dazed.

"Respects to Mrs. Cope. Hope you be back next year. I'd be pleased to see that trailer wagging round the comer with them tent-poles sticking out. That's the way to enjoy life."

I put the letter in my letter-case, and the next day I went back to New York. Charley, for whatever reason, had not spoken of it to Katherine. Every one has a separate kind of reserve, and men, I have noticed, are coy about telling big news; the bigger it is the more they wait to digest it, or not to seem to brag of it, perhaps.

I said to him: "If we'd had any real imagination we might have guessed that ourselves; that trial might have set us thinking. What do you suppose it will do to him?"

"Show him up," he replied.

In a few days, before I had found a good moment for telling Katherine and asking her what she thought of romance and the nineteenth century now, a second letter came with the Vallevista postmark and this was from Tony himself:

My dear General Cope:

I enclose a cutting from a San José paper which will explain what a singular thing has happened to me. I am thrusting my affairs upon you because I feel in need of some advice. You know I have but few friends, but even if I had many it would be to you I should turn. If you will let me say this, Sir, I think of you as the most sensible and the most unworldly man I have ever known. My friend Doctor Allen was a perfectly unworldly man, but he had not seen so much of the world as you have, and on the question of money he was, I think, a little inclined to be narrow, fanatical.

I have never thought much about property—how much one has a right to own, anything like that. I have never thought about this land as property. It sounds all right to say that a great property is a trust, but who can say he is the man to be trusted with it? Nobody would ever pick me out to own this ranch and I should not be likely to choose myself. But certainly I shouldn't chose Mr. Morehouse's nephews, and it seems to be a case of them or me. Or else the whole thing will go into litigation for years, they say. They tell me, too, that the will is sound; I am legally entitled to its provisions. But I would like to mention some of the grounds on which I hesitate.

I haven't the shadow of a claim, of course; it isn't even the gift of a friend. It's like profiting by spite, an old man's revenge. That might be just a notion; but then, too, I had made other plans. I am getting restless; I would like to see more of the world. It isn't that I don't love this country, but perhaps I'm too easy-going. It is a very simple, narrow life, as I can see; and more land wouldn't, perhaps, make it any broader unless I can broaden myself. On the other hand, such a big thing would be a big responsibility and I dread that very much: even though I should get help and advice and a great deal of education out of it. It makes me feel rather wild when I think of it. It was so easy to see Mr. Morehouse's mistakes—now I should have my own on my mind. Should I crawl from under, as you might say? None of these reasons for and against are meant to do more than show you my uncertainty. But the first thought in my mind was, I will confess, rather a dog-in-the-manger fury at the idea of those nephews getting in here doing some of the things they boast they are going to do. The trial shows how generous they would be and how considerate of others! It makes my blood boil.

Well, that is a poor argument; I don't defend it. What I ask is your advice—and please forgive me if I have no business to trouble you in this way.

"I always thought he could say things; give him time," I remarked after my own reading of the letter. "He never had a chance when he was with me and Katherine."

"It's a remarkable letter—remarkable that he should want to write it. Who it's said to or how it's said doesn't matter," said my husband.

"It's nice his calling my old Indian fighter 'sensible and unworldly.' I don't know that we showed much sense last summer, but we certainly didn't display much of this world's gear. You'll let me show this to Katherine before you answer it? I do want to wait and see what she thinks."

Then, on the impulse of the moment, excited as I was, I broke out with the story of Tony's rejection and the beautiful way he had taken it. "I'm not setting aside your judgment, but what Tony really wants to know is what Katherine would have him do."

"And all this about 'unworldliness'—you count that taffy, do you?"

"Ta, ta! The poor boy is human; did you mark his 'restlessness?' If it's going to bring him any nearer to her, to part them farther—that's what he wants to know. Can *you* tell him?"

"I prefer to take him straight, as he said. If he wants Katherine's advice, he can ask her for it. If he's on terms of proposing to her, he can write her a letter."

Later he said: "You and Katherine would like him to act the hero. I want to see him deliver the goods. Let him take up his job and go to it like a man. Not shilly-shally with scruples about spite-work and let those yellow chaps mess it all up."

"Then you would tell him to keep it?"

"I would keep it in his place. I shall tell him that. I don't know what in thunder he'll do with it, but I trust him more than you do. You're afraid he'll soil himself with that land, and he's afraid of it too. But I like, best of all, his unconsciousness as a witness. He doesn't allude to it: hasn't thought of the possibility of any one's thinking he might have been suborned."

"What's that mean?"

"Bought."

"You needn't waste arguments on me; *I* would have him keep the land, for the fun of 'showing him up'. Somebody's got to own it. But do wait and see what Kathie says. She has the latest point of view. You were fighting Aguinaldo, remember, when all her world of idealists called your men 'assassins' and talked about 'another massacre' in the Philippines."

This was an old score and I had better have held my tongue about idealists. He did not leave it to Katherine. He shot his answer off from his club, poor man, and left us to our own arguments and harangues.

Katherine was more guarded with her father than with me. When we were alone she spoke her mind and with so much feeling, so testily in fact, that I was much amused and edified.

"He was perfect as he was—a shore-man, with nothing but his shore. But a rich shore-man!—plastered all over with contracts, acres and acres on his back—scorching over them in a Cadillac, after those trails where no car can go, thank the Lord. Boo! I hate dad for spoiling him. To think he might have stopped it! ... I wonder if he could?"

"What does that mean?"

"You don't suppose it's possible he could be deep—deeper than we think—that he could want the credit of having hesitated—get the land and dad's blessing too? He must have known what an old sport like dad would say. 'Sensible'—'unworldly'!"

"You mean he wasn't sincere? What are you, child!"

"But what a chance to try a man! By Jove! I would have done it in dad's place. I couldn't have helped it.... No; I don't think he posed deliberately; it isn't in him. You know I don't, mams." She saw that I had taken her insinuation to heart. "But what a situation! And there is that side to it that does puzzle one; the decision of a lifetime in the hands of a man he's known three months. How does he know dad's unworldly?"

"He put it in your hands, as nearly as he could without openly calling you his lady-love. I knew that, and I begged father to wait."

"It was well he didn't. I'd have tested him, if it had cost him the land. I should have found out how much he cared for it at a pinch."

"I'm ashamed of you," said I. But I wondered if the wish to have him proved above suspicion was not at the bottom of her pretended doubts. I could not see how any one reading that letter could accuse the writer of insincerity even by thought.

XIV

Katherine was always busy, but for some days I
seemed to see less of her than usual. I telephoned one
afternoon to know if she were at home and asked her
with mocked formality to come and take a cup of
tea with me. She answered that it looked like mental
telepathy; she had been coming, anyhow.

She came, and greeted me with an odd shame-
faced yet triumphant grin. When tea was made,
she brought out a letter—the hand-writing seemed
strangely familiar, yet I did not recognize it—till I had
seen the postmark, Vallevista.

"I was coming over to show you this. Sorry I
haven't a copy of my own letter."

"Your what!" I cried. "Have you written to Tony?"

"You see, mams; prepare yourself—'Stand
by, Ed'ard Cuttle!'—I had to settle it in my own
mind. I wrote to Tony—fact! I steered right across

167

the Commodore's bows and took the wind of him. Sassy?—but I lost the race. I'm a mortified loser, and I didn't keep the rules. But, see here, woman! you put me up to it—you persuaded me he wanted my—whatever you may call it. I didn't give advice exactly. I told him!"

"Well, well!" was all I could say in answer to these tangled metaphors. Katherine never talked like that unless she were in difficulties with her subject.

"Read the letter."

"What's the use when I don't know what you said to him?"

"I can't give you the words, but—" She took a quick breath and laughed. "It was something like this: I told him he had stood the test beautifully. There wasn't a man I knew, not excepting my own father, who would have thought twice about taking that huge ungodly gift. But such a thing might be done on a splendid impulse and be afterwards repented— regretted. There might be a looking-back. And I asked him to bear with me and with one more test."

"Why did you keep using that word?"

"Why did I, to be sure? Well, you can't be tactful and a missionary at the same time. The fact is, I think I must have been testing myself. You can make what shameful inference you please—I don't know what else got into me. I suppose I wanted to learn how much he was glamoured over in my eyes by all this shower of gold—golden opportunity. I have some imagination, you know; you haven't got all the romance in the family. Anyhow, I did use that word. I called it a test, a deliberate challenge to the best he had in him. Would he show me a man in these days who did hesitate and then became satisfied (I knew what father's answer would be), and having held the gift as his own, could lay it down again for the sake of the greater gift—not taking, but giving up. Would he give up the land and be as he was before, uncompromised—far richer in my eyes than if he were loaded down with all that accidental wealth?"

My daughter can usually lay me low in argument, even though when vanquished I may argue still. I salute her banners of progress—from the rear. But this time she failed to sweep me off my feet.

"And you see no 'swank,' about that?" I withered her. She remained, as to her smile, unwithered. "You think it's nice to use a man's love in that way? You might as well offer him a kiss for his vote."

"Mother, dear, you need not worry about his vote. Read the letter."

… It had no formal opening: it began: "I love you more than ever, but now I do not understand you. We 'test' people we don't quite trust, isn't it so? The word you use about the land—how do you mean I should be compromised? The only meaning to me is that it shows your doubt of my motives in taking it and my ability to use it well. But it isn't the land. There is nothing you could ask that I would not do, or give, if I had it to give, or give up. And I don't wonder you doubt my fitness to handle it. But your letter came too late.

"You know I wrote to your father, not to chat about the matter. I asked his advice and told him my decision was in his hands. He must have understood it so, for he wrote me such a letter as I have never had in my life. It is enough to last me my life. He said: 'You don't want to spend your youth behind the lines; that's the place for the old fellows. This is your front, my son: go to it like a man.' I took it as an order. I can't write to your father now and say I did not mean what I said before and take it back. I would sooner be shot, to tell the truth. So, if your 'test' is a serious one, and if it goes against me, I must lose, even if I lose everything, or wait."

"Good for the 'kitchen knave'!" said I.

"You might as well drop that," said Katherine.

"Yes; he's won his spurs." I snatched another comparison which pleased me better—"You are like the lady who threw her glove to the lions as a 'test,' and you've got it back again—smack in your face. I hope you'll thank him properly."

"I shall," said Katherine, "when I get to France."

She could not have realized the shock she was giving me. We were in such close proximity and sympathy, each fancied the other must know without words what was heading up in her own mind. I knew, as a fact, no more about her plans for France than she knew about my wakeful nights thinking of Cecily and Peter. I asked if she could be spared from her work here?

"Anybody can be spared," she answered impatiently. "I go on Helen's money and some one who hasn't any Helen or any money will take my job and do it better than I did. Helen can't be spared; she's an organizer; she's needed at G.H.Q. It's beginning to roll up and it's a huge, big thing—this country is going to get to France somehow. Well, mams, dear, you wouldn't hold back a son? We thrashed this all out before. It isn't a question of here or there or what one does; one must do something."

There were no more arguments, of course; I could make a chapter of our talks that avoided argument. Once she said (during her packing): "It's odd—Helen and I have always said we found each other in France. In England we scrapped a little; she takes everything English just as it comes—adores them and all their ways. Some of those tall, beautiful male beings were almost too like their own caricatures in 'Punch.' Most of them dead now—such deaths, my soul! And we American girls could laugh at them! But in France we were two hearts that beat as one. Well, I go back—on Helen's money once more. We revisit France together. If there's anything left to laugh at, I shall laugh for two, and cry for two."

"For three," said I. "But will you ever write me real letters? You'll be so rushed; and when you have any time to rest you must rest. But—I may as well face it—this is our first actual parting. All the little things you used to write I shall miss, the little nothings just between us two. I shall never know, I suppose, what you are going to say to Tony. And he's my Tony, though I tossed him to you to play with."

I had a pencil with which I had been checking up a laundry-bill. She took it out of my hand and on the margin of an old slip she wrote one word, wrote it large so I could read it without my spectacles: "Wait."

XV

Helen gave an exquisite little dinner for Katherine and dared to ask only girls; this was on the eve of her going to France. We called it, because Katherine's parents were the only "male-and-female-created-he-them" persons present, a third-sex dinner. We had unsexed wine, too, but were easily elevated by each other's nonsense—their nonsense; Charley and I did not speak the language of these wonderful, super-civilized young goddesses which our latest times have evolved. Looking at them in their intelligence and grace and power, and the self-confidence that perfect form, manner, social background gives, their superb health and in some cases beauty, in all of them a certain soul-attitude of large, living experience that made ancients of an old army couple like us;—well, it made me long to swear!—for I said to myself, "The ungrateful hussies, they will not marry!" As a matter of fact, one or two of them are since married; but by way of argument it is plain such girls cannot marry under terms not obtainable short of a new planet, or this old one made over according to their ideas. Most men as their husbands would have had to sit dumb and smiling blankly, as my old husband did under the volleys of their rapid-fire, allusive, hyperbolical talk. Some of it was shop, but such clever tongues and turns, inventing as they ran! It made me think of the ground-fires that lick along the floor of an old forest and leap up a giant tree-bole now and then, turning its towering aloofness into a beacon-flare. So would they soar to the height of an occasional grand and alarming idea. I can't say but that many of these ideas that stunned me had been borrowed from bigger fires of genius—they were all reading the new Frenchmen, the Internationalists; and many of them, seated there in family jewels and gowns of rank price, were rank socialists themselves, prepared, in theory at least, to go in khaki and fling those jewels into the common heap. It was when they discounted the "My Country" idea that Charley and I groaned aloud: he admitted that he would have had to add, when it came to orders, "My country right or wrong"; and here they groaned at him in a chorus of lamentation and prophecy. And after dinner they all smoked together in peace, and there was music—of the present, to them, which to me was decidedly of the future if at all! I made a feeble clutch at Debussy who came nearest to my understanding, to the extent, at least, of being rather excited by him (as a dog might howl). But as to pleasure—they were not deceived. Sarah Huntwell, Katherine's husband, was the musician; she beamed at me over her shoulder and slid into the Barcarole from "Love Tales," and there were smiles at the old lady from the ocean shore of the most robustly romantic State in the Union. They were not scorners of romance in the very young or the aged; they allowed us our toys. And my old soldier-man, whose politics they condoned because he was a toothless old lion, and whose nationalism to them was a collection of ancient symbols—himself they cajoled to the top of their bent as personally a perfect dear. And so it went, between our time gone by and theirs immediate and urgent, with all our postponed problems unsolved and our bad work to undo. Privately, Charley and I thanked our stars we were born before this deluge.

Helen was very lovely to us after Katherine went, but she was much occupied. All these girls were unconscionably busy. I was inducted into a unit of war-workers and sewed at a long tableful of women two afternoons a week. But many of my afternoons were, as one says, my own. Having lived so long with men, American men who have no tea-hour, I had never set up one for myself; usually at that time I went for a solitary walk. Even a city solitude rested me more than anything except a good book, and Charley with another good book, silently smoking beside me.

But why should I need rest? Because one's thoughts may tire one a little, and letters from her

children are events of tantalizing importance to a
mother, who never feels that she knows all and is
powerless, if she did know, either to help or hinder. If
one were lying on beds of asphodel and one's children
were still in the stream of life, those Elysian dreams
would not be very deep.

Week by week my letters were coming, from
Cecy in San Francisco, from Patty in the Philippines,
and from Katherine in France. Patty had brought
a little red-headed grandson into the family and
named him Charles Cope Gallagher. Privately, in our
bigoted fashion we deplored the "Gallagher," though
the introducer of that name, and of the red hair,
had turned out extremely well, had made good both
as an officer and a son-in-law, while Peter, with the
dark-brown locks and ornamental surname, we were
ashamed to talk of.

As to the letters, Patty's were normal. (This was
our word always for Patty.) They meant, in general,
peace of mind and simple cares and satisfactions, and
were singularly removed from the Great War. Cecily's
were almost as much so, though she did things with
her pretty hands, gave money, I inferred; but in
everything she said I felt the constrained consciousness
of a woman humiliated, hardening herself and playing
a part. She did not say that Peter never wrote; she
no longer spoke of him at all. This last shock had
come when she had been off her guard through
love's weakness, not its strength; Peter had left her no
protection but pride and silence. I thought her silence

quite wonderful in a woman of what I should call her caliber, but its reactions gave me keen fears for my own child.

About this time, in the natural sequence of small events whose outcome one never can guess, Tony Kayding's name began to repeat itself in her letters. He had written that he was planning to build on the shore and asked if we could recommend him an architect. He wrote from San Francisco and we referred him to Cecily, enclosing a letter to introduce him. She had handed him over to the man of her selection, Ralph Robbins, and both young men had been her guests, more than once, Tony keeping up his visits ingenuously without much thought of the conventions. All the fussy little details which Katherine's letters would have left out, Cecily gave, with none of her own thoughts or her concrete state of mind. She told me, for example, what her new dresses were. Hobble-skirts were doing their worst that winter, but she declared gayly that whatever the fashion said "went" with her, which I had observed myself. The letters were full of little heart-breaking frivolities; her mother knew how much of this was bravado. One cannot confess grief or accept sympathy for a husband as cynically recreant as Peter—following other strains on her loyalty and forbearance. I had begged for long and frequent letters, alleging my loneliness; I am never lonely, in fact, but I knew it would be good for us both, this winter of all winters of our lives, to keep in as close touch as possible.

But her letters I read by the rule of contraries: when she spoke constantly and with enthusiasm of Tony, I knew she was not absorbed in him: he was merely another means of passing the time. Cecy's comments upon him were not deep; they were hurried, makeshift remarks and sometimes wanting in dignity. I did not value from her the information that he had shaved his mustache and that Emilia Curtis (one of Cecy's friends who read Browning and was rather proud of it) said he looked like the young priest in "The Ring and the Book." I thought it quite likely the comparison might be apt, but I did not send that letter on to Katherine. In fact, I sent very few of Cecy's letters. Katherine could not understand (though she might guess) the bitter excuse there was in my mind always for their jarring triviality. And I did not show them to her father—those letters in which Tony was in this way flattered.

Katherine's letters, while they were short and no longer conversational, were like the moments in which they were written; they were the recoil of an empty piece from which the explosive had been fired. And some of them hit me almost as hard. I used to put on my things and go for a fast walk, to work off the shivering excitement they caused in me. Others expressed by their very blankness how dead-tired the writer had been; "I will tell you some day, but not now."

In short, Patty, our happy child, comforted our hopes in the future; Katherine's future I could not see;

Cecily we did not talk of. A few of her letters I did show, of course (they weren't all filled with Tony). Her father would hand them back without allowing me to see his eyes.

XVI

I had ventured out one April afternoon on the edge of a thunderstorm, having forgotten what they are like in the old home climate. It overtook me as I was hurrying back across the square. A man's step came striding fast behind me, and I hoped it might belong to some good soul with an umbrella who would offer me half. A hand and arm held out the umbrella; I looked up to thank, as I supposed, a stranger, into Peter's face, Peter Dalbert entrapped through an act of kindness. This might be called a good omen, but not as Peter took it.

The change in his expression when he saw with whom he was linked up, threw me into hysterical laughter. We could not speak; the storm came swashing down. I clutched his arm and bent before the rush of wind and rain, trusting he did not know what shook me. I could not pretend to be weeping, though I did try to wipe my face. The clouds above us did not meet with more of an electric shock than my contradictory feelings in this encounter. I wanted to get rid of him, and yet I knew I must see him and see this meeting through. His own mortified surprise showed how pleased he was to see me! We staggered on, and I halted him in front of our little hotel on the south side of the square. It was an hour when I am usually alone and I asked him to come in. He demurred as I expected; I would take no refusal.

"Do come in. I want to thank you, when I get my breath…. We must have another talk…. Well; perhaps you oughtn't to stop: you're very wet, aren't you? You gave me all your umbrella!"

This, I think, actually turned the scale; like a proud school-boy, he could not brook the supposition that he had been uneasy about taking cold. We went up together in our small elevator, to our rooms which have no sun in the afternoon. I ordered a fire in the sitting-room, Peter protesting, "Not for me."

"For me, then," said I, "and the tea for us both. Do you ever drink tea?"

"Tea's quite all right," said Peter condescendingly. "I'm just over from London, you know."

"On your way to San Francisco?"

"I'm starting out there to-morrow or day after."

I made no comment. He was darkly civil, set out the tea-table and opened its leaves and brought my chair. We were silent watching the kettle begin to sing.

"Peter, don't you think you've been rather impossible this winter?" I opened my offensive cautiously. "What do you suppose your 'absent treatment' has done to Cecily?"

"Ah," he exclaimed: "I've come back to see about Cecily! From all reports she hasn't missed me much."

"Why haven't you written to her? Do you go by hearsay when it's your wife?"

Peter pushed his chair back from the fire. "You intimated that I was too 'vile' to touch her. So I did the other thing—put the ocean between us. Then it was up to you to do the explaining."

"You did this to get even with me? Well, Peter; so far as I am able to explain you, you remain unexplained. And now what next?"

"It's not Peter's case now; it's Peter's wife," he retorted. "Have you heard of a friend of hers named Kayding?"

"If I were Cecy's father," I said softly, "and you spoke of her like that! ... Well, we'll have our tea before we discuss Tony Kayding. I think you and Germany get your 'reports' from the same kind of sources and they mislead you. You leave out the 'imponderables.'"

"Is this fellow you call 'Tony,' is he an imponderable?"

"In the sense that he would be difficult for you to understand, yes. He's a great friend of ours. We introduced him to Cecy."

"And he's suddenly got a lot of money—is that an imponderable?"

"I don't see how it affects the case; but, yes; he's building a house and she introduced him to Ralph Robbins: without money, I suppose he couldn't afford Ralph Robbins."

"I know all that. And they trot round the shops like newly-weds looking at curtains and wall-paper. Why does my wife have to furnish his house for him? He's there so much that everybody's talking. Is that true, or isn't it?"

"It is true he's there a good deal; but it's you who have set people talking. That's no argument for Tony though. What saves a man's name and a woman's, is the woman and the man. You ought to know your own wife a little; has she ever been silly about any man but you? Tony goes there too often, very likely; he's a guileless person—he's not like any man you've ever known, or that we have, but there's no one who doesn't trust him. Cecy's father has backed him for a good deal more than a mere introduction implies; I don't mean money—just pure faith."

"And she trusts him like a saint, too, I suppose?— and gives him a saint's privileges."

"I don't know what a saint's privileges are, unless martyrdom is one of them.... Peter, if you go back there, after this winter, in this coarse, sneering state of mind, stuffed full of vulgar gossip—"

"'Vulgar'—what! I have inside information, remember."

"Inside or outside, you ought to be ashamed of it. You will not be able to keep your meanness to yourself:

Cecy will know that you've had her watched while you were hiding your own life. That is unforgivable. She is holding on to what faith she can keep in you, with nothing to hide, while you've been dodging in the dark setting spies on her. Before you lay charges, make your own record clear. It is you who are on trial as a husband, not she as a wife.... Will you have another cup?"

Peter handed his empty cup. His hand shook; his face was aflame with wind and fire-heat. I hoped a little of that burning red might have come from within.

"If you want to know what I've been doing,"—he threw down his mask with childish violence,—"I've been in the dirt where you said I belonged."

"What an extraordinary statement! You know I never could have said that."

"What does 'vile' mean?"

"It doesn't mean dirt necessarily. What do *you* mean by 'dirt'?"

"Call it a shell-factory, what? Been makin' munitions—stokin' up the war."

He had counted on my surprise, which I did not conceal, but seeing he expected praise as well, I hardened my heart. I simply remarked we had hoped he was in France, but could get no trace of him there.

"I'm sick of France! Every other man I know is over there doing the hero-job—ask you a lot of questions! I went where not a beggar knew me from Adam. Bully chaps and women too. I made good, you know." He displayed his hands. "They were a bunch of bread-winners all right. Mind you, a good mechanic was spoiled in me."

He made way with a quantity of innocuous "educators"—all I had to offer him without fuss. His appetite seemed not at all impaired by the nature of our talk. "Let me tell you; I'd sooner be in a shell-factory than a London club just now. It's not pleasant to be an American in England, or any man of fighting age if he's not in khaki. No; it wasn't bad, not half bad."

"And are you back here only because of these 'reports' about Cecy, do I understand?"

"Oh, I know you aren't glad to see me; and that's why I didn't let Cecy know I was coming, so she could have told you."

"You still imagine I am plotting a divorce? Can't you reason that if I were I should *want* you to go back with all this stuff in your mind and insult her after you have wrung her heart? That would finish it. And perhaps it's time it was finished. When you have destroyed her love, your own, from what I have seen of it, would hardly be worth saving."

Peter eyed me with his old hardihood. He grasped the sincerity with which I spoke of Cecy's love as a thing still alive, and not to be doubted. And still he might spoil all.… "Well, say! Suppose I don't go back. What sort of a goat would you like to make of me? What do you want me to do?"

"My advice doesn't combine well with your way of taking it. But if you ask me what I think, I think you have done well enough with your hands, but dirt on your hands won't save you. What is a 'gentleman-ranker'! Go where they *do* know you and will ask you questions. Go and get a soul started somehow. People seem to find their souls in France. Go and see death, and perhaps you may learn something about life."

His face changed; there was a short and I was fain to think an encouraging silence. "I'll go to France, then, if it's going to make everybody so happy. You think I'm afraid of death. Well, we'll see! But now you've come between us again—if I can't see her what's the matter with my seeing some of her letters? Hasn't she written to you this winter?"

Was this cunning on his part? I was staggered, and temporizing did not help. All the black thoughts he had fed on I could see stick up their ugly heads as he watched my hesitation.

"Peter, things that aren't meant for us never do us any good. Letters are to one person; there's no surer way to make trouble than to pass them around. You haven't any business with my letters, and under the circumstances I have no business to show them. Cecy's life has not been normal this winter; that's your fault; and her letters are not good evidence of her thoughts and feelings. I understand them, but you may not."

He was silent a moment. "I see; the fact is you're afraid to show them. They don't bear out what you have claimed."

"They certainly do not bear out my belief that Cecy loves you—more than you deserve. All the first ones were written under the sting of your neglect, to persuade me that she was not crushed by it. She has some spirit. Then Katherine went to France and she wrote to comfort me. When you are thinking of another's pain you hide your own. Tony Kayding was introduced to her about that time and she wished to show her pleasure in the acquaintance, as we brought it on her."

I could never be sure that Peter followed my meaning, and I found myself always repeating and elaborating the simplest statement. "Now, this is the key to her letters partly, but you'll forget it as soon as you begin your search—for that is what it is, if you persist. There is green in your eye, and you'll read things into her innocent words that are not there. Put it this way: suppose you had died really, and were using what we imagine may be the power of the dead, to look back at her, yourself invisible—Do you follow me? Suppose you wanted to satisfy yourself of the genuineness of her grief. You might catch her in front of a mirror trying on a new hat, or eating candy or laughing with her friends; no sign of grief about her but her black clothes. If the dead, or the sham-dead, want to try these one-sided experiments they've only their own suspicious vanity to thank if they get a shock. If you *dare* to read those letters you may have them; but I am sorry for you."

Peter's face was redder than ever. He blinked. "I take the risk. You can't bluff me, Mrs. Cope."

"Very well, then. Come to-morrow about ten. I must ask you to read them here."

"Oh; you can't trust me with my wife's letters!"

"They are my letters. And I don't trust you, naturally: why should I?"

We were both hot with anger now; Peter's next speech was quite indecent. "I suppose you'll go over them and cut out all the risky ones."

"You are a wretched, unhappy boy. You shall have them all, to the last one!"

That night I went over my poor girl's letters and saw that only the "risky" ones were left. The ones I had best liked, the womanly ones with the right tone, I had sent over to Katherine. It was a dastardly demand of Peter's, but he would get his punishment promptly; it was plain what he would imagine here. It was possible to draw back even now, and refuse to allow my letters to be used as proofs of what cannot be questioned; men who ask to see your letters are put out of the game. In one way, however, it was too late; I was worn out with Peter. It was a trap of his own setting; let him walk into it and suffer the consequences.

There were allusions he would not understand who never read anything, dippings from wells that were not deep, but were too deep for Peter; playful nothings impossible to explain to one whose vanity was ready to be stung and whose imagination would be sure to lead him into the mire. One instance is enough, and I give it, though it is hard on my poor child:

"Tony Kayding was here to tea with R. R.—my day at home. He prefers to come when it isn't my day, but this time he was caught. He had on a new frock coat et cetera, correct even to his spats. He has really a respect for the conventions, only he doesn't know what they are. I am teaching him the proper way to give a lady a 'light,' a thing that never entered his consciousness before. And do you remember an old book called 'The Dolly Dialogues'? Well, I am 'Dolly,' in his case; the other day I actually found myself showing him how to fold his umbrella!—which he had dreamily brought into the drawing-room. I shall be able to say with Dolly, 'I made that man!' And then I suppose he'll go off and fall in love, and not see me when we pass in the street. But for all he's so grateful and docile as my society-pupil, he will suddenly stop short at some trifle, a manicure, for instance. But his hands are so perfect he doesn't need one. Did you ever see such hands on a man who dresses as he—did! When you see him now you will stare! He looks like an Italian prince. The girls are all wild about him; they are trying to get up some theatricals on purpose to ring him in; for he isn't easy to flirt with. I wonder where he gets his poise? Is he religious? Has he had a 'disappointment'? He's in tip-top health, going strong in his ranch affairs. Is he chasing the dollars? He'll turn away from a pretty girl and talk to some old professor person from Berkeley to ask about fertilizers or how to cure bugs in a bean-crop.

"Here I've written a whole sheet about him. Well, he's the most interesting new man in town this winter. Glad you sent him."

Peter came next morning punctual to the hour. His mind was not changed, I saw, and very likely he recognized in my manner to him the same settled disgust. He went at his letters and I took up my knitting. I do not knit without looking on and I could not follow the expressions of his face, but I gathered the poison was beginning to work. The letters were arranged according to their dates, with those breaks I have spoken of where a good one was missing. He hurried through the earlier ones to follow like a sleuth the name of Kayding, after it appeared: Ralph Robbins's delighted epigrams about his new client, Cecily's exclamations that he was charming, and why hadn't we said more about him when we knew him down at the shore? I caught now and then the sound of a deep breath, or he fidgeted in his chair, and at last he sprang up with one word, "Damn!"—and started for the fire with the letter he had been reading crushed in his hand.

"What are you doing?" I warded. "You can't burn my letters!"

"What's this 'Dolly' rot— will you tell me?"

"Be civil, please. I really can't tell you. She's a character in a book."

"What sort of character?"

"Good-natured, for one thing. She helped a *gauche* young man to improve himself socially, brought him out—'made' him."

"Did she rave about his hands and call him an Italian prince?"

I went on with my knitting, remarking to myself (I was pretty reckless by now)—

"'Them that takes cakes
Which the Parsee-man bakes
Makes dreadful mistakes.'"

Peter returned to his "cakes." He had taken up the last letter, and very soon (to mix metaphors) I knew the trap would be sprung. Ralph Robbins and Tony had made up a party to motor down the coast to inspect the new house now well up on its foundations. Cecily had not seen it before. Nor, until I read this letter, had I known the site Tony had chosen; it was a surprise to both Charley and me. We did not know that he knew we had given up our dream of a home on that spot. It was our own Point he was building on. To me the coincidence was so strange that it amounted to a shock, that Tony, all unconscious, guided and assisted by Cecy, should have joined us there—Peter and me and the ghost. I remember, as I read, I felt as if a cold finger were laid upon my spine.

It was a party of four: Ralph Robbins, Emilia Curtis (the girl who read Browning), Tony driving his own car, and Cecy in the seat of honor. They were to pass our old campground and so down three miles to the field, the gate into the field and the house, its west windows looking down at our trysting-place.

Peter, when he came, as it were to the gate of that field, sat very still; I heard the paper rattle. After a moment we both looked up. His eyes are not very expressive, but as they met mine they had the stare of a hard-breathed creature at bay.

"You contrived this: you put him up to choose that place. It couldn't have happened without help."

"I was struck with that thought, myself; but it wasn't my help! Ghosts are lonely, perhaps; they may like company."

"You don't believe me, but I was getting ahead on that score. A man can't be much of a bird and live on the sweat of his brow and chuck his income to the war-orphans; that's what I did last winter."

"Pride goes before a fall, Peter. Why did you degrade it all by this last breach of honor?"

"You can't think of things when you're fighting mad! I'm going to try again. But will there be anything left when I come back?"

"As much as you deserve, I think. Will you write to her, faithfully—and will you stop those lies behind her back?"

"Lies?" he repeated mechanically. "Cut out my own mother's letters!"

The tragic boy! He had done precisely what I feared, when he went up to Tahoe; told the proud, unhappy woman a half-truth, made himself out a victim chased away by his mother-in-law. What mother would not have fought, though some might not have chosen those weapons! She had been preparing counter-charges in face of the claim she expected we would bring: this was her fight for the grandsons. It was of her I thought, not of myself, when I said, "How can any one help you when you will not act square?"

"God in Heaven!" he turned on me, "who asked your help?"

"Who," said I, "put your miserable secrets in my hands? I had no desire to pry into your sins; they may seem to you an interesting scarlet—they don't interest me. Now, we'll part company, if we can: you and I and the ghost of that woman at the Point."

"O God, leave the woman alone! What do you know of men like me? You don't even know how little such things count."

"There is where you make your eternal mistake. 'Morale' is the only thing that does count. If you can't face death without it, how can you face life—and the greatest lesson of life? Well; you must learn it your own way. I'm sorry I ever wasted good anger on you."

Peter had one sporting quality—he might be said to "come back" after a lashing. He drew in his breath hard. "I believe I will go out there. I've some things to say to Cecy myself. Not to stay—after that I'll lug stretchers, anything." He looked at me in a pause which might have been a question. I remained silent.

He rose and quietly laid the last letter with the others on the table at my side. There was a chair near, and he sat and rested his elbow on the table and held out his hand. I did not accept it at once. I looked in his eyes first. There was shame in them, I thought, and even a suspicion of tears. "I won't stay but a week. A man can't be much of a damned fool in one week."

The next evening came a telegram: "Terms accepted. Good-bye." … At bedtime I went over Cecy's letters again and burned all those relating to Tony's social success in San Francisco. I was extremely tired of that episode myself, and only wished I had burned them before. Then I remembered the moral of the cakes (that the Parsee-man bakes). Possibly Peter needed just those crumbs inside his thick hide of self-satisfaction.

XVII

There came a break about this time in my letters from Cecily which corresponded to the date of Peter's visit. That week she did not write. The weather for April was unusually warm; soft sea-winds blowing up Broadway and violets for sale on the street-corners, as I remembered when I was a girl. Charley took to walking home from his club and he never failed to bring me a bunch. All our talks were violet-scented, though they were practical enough. We read less evenings and sat out on the narrow city balcony which our windows opened on, he smoking, I trying feebly to knit by the light of a neighboring street-lamp. The leafless magnolias in the square had opened their white, lamplike flowers and all the tree-buds were swelling and turning to jewels in the evening light. Sunsets in spring have peculiar memories for any woman who once was a girl in New York.

"What about this summer?" I asked when day after day passed and no hint of future plans escaped my spouse. "Do we go West again and unpack the camp-stuff?"

"Think you aren't tired of the old shore?"

"Are you?" said I "The only question is, don't we feel a little as Katherine did? Isn't it pretty far from the war? I wonder if we could stand it another summer to listen to that ground-swell?" As I spoke, we seemed to hear it in the roar of the city, distant, subdued to us in our dim, shadowy precinct lined with old houses of the past. "Do you think we could spend another summer just fishing and reading and walking the shore-path and writing letters?"

"No, I don't; and that's why I have something to tell you." After a provoking interval of silence, he resumed. "Kayding thinks, you know—that he wants me to help him out there on the ranch. Wants me to be his 'resident manager.'"

"What!" I cried, prolonging my vowel.

"Well, yes! Sounds like a practical joke—Hands me back the same quandary he was in. I advise him to keep the land and he retaliates, 'then come out here and help me run it'; and names a price that I'm ashamed to tell you."

"Tony doesn't see that he's paying you for your advice any more than he saw he was being paid for his testimony. You like his unconsciousness—can't you be unconscious too?"

"No, I can't, but I will. That's what I wanted to know: are you satisfied?"

"Why, yes; the thing makes one laugh. I've some sense of humor."

"Well, don't have too much or you'll ruin the job for me. It takes nerve to go in for it without a blush."

"What we can stand in each other we needn't blush for outside. I've got reasons of my own for blushing right in the family if you did but know. I had a horrid visit last fall; and I can't tell you about it."

"Any time Cecy wants to get rid of that fellow, let her come to me; till then I don't care what he does with himself nor where he keeps himself, and if you know you needn't tell me. Now, I want to get busy up to the hilt. For a year or two, perhaps, I could hold down Tony's job; by that time he'll shoulder it himself or he'll have found the right man in my place."

"You can build that road with culverts!" We recalled our tent-dinner and agreed that the nonsense we talked that evening seemed no more unreal than these plans we were actually making now. As, for example, I asked, "Where is the 'resident manager' going to live? I suppose we can't be gypsies any more; a man of business must have a house or an office?"

"I wonder—if you could manage in a corner of that—hotel?" he finished with a craven smile. "If you were inside you wouldn't see the outside."

"Perhaps you've never seen the inside!" We were both laughing now; but it looked as if it might be our only choice, the hotel or the town—we could do things to the inside, Charley said, adding the timely compliment that he'd seen me make a home out of worse quarters.

"Not bigger! Size counts in a job of that kind." But for us to build now would be folly, we agreed. My old soldier-man had his eye, I knew, on the active list if we should break into the war or be dragged in. I asked him once more and for the thousandth time if he believed we ever should be?

"If we don't we'll go into the discard," he growled.

If we hadn't been so on in life and so meek in our retiracy, we should have felt in this new turn that we were the sport of fate, hauled out of our obscurity and pointedly taken notice of. The irony of it (one of the ironies), that after so kindly patronizing Kayding all last summer and calling ourselves his fate, we should now be eating out of his hand in earnest!

Charley owned to me that he was keen for the job. He saw a hundred possibilities ahead to one that he would ever see finished in all likelihood, but it was something, as he said, to start the show.

I said: "You'll be singing together like morning stars in the dawn of your creations, but that doesn't settle where we are to live. I'm like the woman when everything was 'wild,' I want a nice dry cave and a curtain to my cave."

"There shall be curtains—you can go up and stay with Cecy and buy some while we lay out our schemes. I'll be back and forth and keep you posted."

All this was enough to occupy one's thoughts, and the week flew. At the beginning of the next week a thick letter came from Cecily. I quailed as I ran over the mass of sheets in Cecily's large handwriting, sentences dashed across page after page. The silence was broken between us. My poor child's words drummed on my heart like a noise of guns:

"Mother, I must speak at last. Don't imagine you know anything about my life this winter from my letters to you. You haven't the least idea! No one has dared to ask me about my husband. I did not know whether I should ever see him again. But this I decided: if he came back expecting me to fall on his neck or at his feet!—he'd be mistaken. The worm has turned. I am not anxious for a divorce; why should he step off jauntily and leave me the humiliation and the talk? Every one blames the wife; it's always her fault. This, of course, supposing he should come back and want to make up as he has done so often, saying I was the 'only one.' The only one! Did father ever tell you after you were his wife and our mother that you were the only one!

"Well, he came back, as you know. He dashed out here just off his train. It was nine o'clock, and I expected him—he had wired. And at first sight of him I saw he was just the same to me, and that in the old way that I'm ashamed of, I was the same to him. I was the 'only one' after all. After what?

"I couldn't be cold to him, though I was pretty passive. He's the very same, just as he was the day, the hour before he went to Tahoe and disappeared for seven months without a word. He was just as fond of me then—don't you remember how happy I thought I was? Why should I trust him now? He's made so that he doesn't show dirt—not yet. He asked if he wasn't 'all right'—as to drinking, which I could see he was. More than that he wouldn't say a word. But expected me to take him back into my life as my husband, knowing nothing about his life since I saw him last. I said, 'You might be any man—you are a stranger to me. A stranger you may stay.' I don't know how I had the strength to say it—he's not a stranger! But this can't be marriage. I asked him what did he think marriage meant?

"What a fool, what a baby I must have been! He was simply astounded that I should make terms with him instead of dressing up to be kissed and forgive and forget. Mother, now I understand *you*. I don't know how you dared to do it, but I can't say it may not have been the only way; he took it all wrong because he was all wrong himself, but I think it started things, it was the entering wedge.

"He would never have confessed to you the most shameful part, but he did to me. And for this reason: to prove how little he cared for women of that kind! He confessed the fact that he didn't *care* when she went down; she was a horrible nuisance and he loathed her. He might have saved her, with danger to himself, and he wouldn't take that risk for her more than if she had been a dog. No wonder he had to do something straight off—love his wife better, stop drinking, anything! He was afraid to think. He was pursued. He said he fought against it, but the thing was always before his eyes—that moment when he *looked and saw he was not there alone*. You called him a coward. He denied that, but he owned the other—that her death might have been prevented.

"In all the years I have known him I've never once seen him sorry for anything he had done. Disgusting scenes after drinking—he'd sulk, refuse to speak, and be very haughty and absurd. He was a stone, and a shifty stone; you never knew where he'd be next. That night, if you can believe it, he went down at my knees and sobbed with his head in my lap. He hadn't known, he said, how much I was to him. And I sent him away—after that. Because I have trusted and trusted— Never again. Without proofs. I haven't asked anything very hard of him, simply to take a little trouble to show that out of sight is not out of mind. Only to write me a husband's letters. That is all I demanded by way of proof. You may see I have not been a pampered wife. He never writes to me! He hates to write—he telegraphs. Now he will write or he needn't come back. Do you call that much to ask?

"He thought it terribly hard of me to send him away that night (it was morning; we talked till two o'clock). I couldn't send him out of his own house, but he knew the conditions if he stayed. They were what you demanded, if I understood him? He respects you in a raging sort of way. Do you know what I wish you would do—for me? Do you think you could write to him after a while, when he gets over to France? Just as if he were your 'godson.' Some of those godsons, perhaps, are no better than he, if we did but know it. Just because you seared him so deep, I think it would give him a brace if you would write to him now as if he were one of the others over there. It gives me a wild sort of hope to have seen him actually moved—galled by what you said and by what I knew he must think of himself. It was because he didn't want to think, that he got into that factory among all the noise and away from anybody who could talk to him about home. But now that he has forced himself to tell, even the very worst, I believe he will feel like a different man. I'm so glad you called him a coward! He'd rather be a murderer. Of course he was both, you will say. You may say anything now! But will you write to him? There must be bad lives over there, lives that have been wasted till now;—they make just as good a sacrifice, when they are given away.

"Mother, dear, I love you as I never could before, because I could not be open with you; I had too much to be ashamed of. I did know about Peter—about his drinking—before I married him, but I thought in the pride of my heart that I could change him, and I was so silly about him, anyhow, that I didn't care. You have suffered for me without the comfort of being able to speak.… Oh, another thing to his credit! He gulped down his jealousy of Tony Kayding which he couldn't hide, and I took no trouble to contradict things; I said there were men the girls he admired were crazy about who were good and manly, too. He denies that we ever can tell about them; no man, he says, is pure. I saw that jealousy was a part of his pleading now for my love again, and that is another reason why I will not trust him without these slow, tiresome proofs that mean unselfishness. Let him *do* something for me that bores him, and do it constantly, even such a little thing as to write me letters when he'd rather go to sleep and needs to sleep."

Cecy, as her own mother knew, was not a worm, and she was not one of those long-suffering wives of old who let themselves be dragged after the triumphal car of man's selfishness and vanity. She had her own share of girlish vanity, and I had never observed that she was unselfish. I cared now scarcely at all for her happiness; but I believed that for her as a woman, as well as for Peter as a man, the best hope in the future lay in changing the character of the bond between them, not in breaking it. I wanted to see her lift her ideal of marriage so it should clear the ground on which she had been able to accept him hitherto, even though with scorn for the compromise. This she had begun to do; if now she could go on, and if Peter had the stuff in him for any real response!

And so I made my visit to her, more satisfied than I had been for years. I had borne up wincing under her over-emphasized admiration for Tony; now, since her letter, it had fallen into the background of my thoughts—the last thing I had expected to "worry" about. Yet here it was again, a flourishing fact before every one's eyes. Tony came too often, unless it had been to see me, which most evidently it was not. It seemed to be by appointment he came, and he and Cecy, after a few moments' chat, would excuse themselves and go off on some one of their numerous errands together — always practical; sometimes war-work, or Belgian Relief; but oftener it was the old subject of the new house, Tony's. A mother is not a guest to be treated with ceremony; still, I thought they were behaving in a tasteless manner and Tony's social education seemed to have a false root somewhere.

Was I becoming a jealous old woman insisting on my own importance? I could have willingly admitted this sooner than be forced to see the young ones, in whom it supremely mattered, in such an unbecoming light. Tony sometimes would look at me in the old, serious, gentle way but nothing serious in words ever came of it. Never once did he mention Katherine. I certainly was jealous for her! I kept her grimly to myself.

"What are you in pursuit of to-day?" I asked, not very sweetly, one afternoon when Cecy, hatted and gloved, with her coat on the back of a chair, stood at the window waiting for Tony.

"Oh," she sighed, and laughed; "it's still a question of old rose. Personally I think it's a mistake for a man's bedroom."

"What man's bedroom?"

"Tony's—the new house. What do you think of it?"

"If he wants old rose, I should let him have it; it's none of my affair," I answered shortly.

"But he wants me to get it for him—his curtains and all the rest of it, and there's a great deal of difference in old rose."

"How does he know the difference!" I sneered. "You should have seen where he lived last summer. His sitting-room was painted chocolate, with old boots and soiled newspapers lying around, and not a curtain or a window-shade anywhere. He was much nicer then than he is now."

"But tell me, anyhow, what you think?"

"About what, my dear?"

"Old rose," Cecy kept at me maddeningly.

"I think it's an old granny's color—old rose and ashes of roses. And he's an old granny himself to make such a fuss over nothing."

It flashed upon me while speaking that I must be talking nonsense; Tony was not an old granny nor different in any way except that he wore better clothes; nor had he developed softening of the brain. There must be something underneath this calculating and conspicuous foolishness and persistence. I was always too hasty—And now I recalled how once or twice when we had driven down to the Point, Tony and Katherine had escorted us and stayed awhile and ridden on; they must often have been there by themselves. How if the

Point were a trysting-place for him too—with a loved
and living ghost? A light of great joy broke in. This was
Katherine's house! He had been using one sister's taste
to help him plan a house for the real one, who would
not talk or think of houses. Yet Katherine must have
sent him his word that she had confided to me, firmly,
though on a scrap of paper. Katherine did not scrap her
words. I hauled in my horns and was content.

"Do you and Katherine like old rose?" I inquired
subtly.

"I can't bear it! But Tony is set on old rose for
his bedroom, and nothing all over the house but
pale tints—a water-color house, rather bare, but very
delicate; not a man's house at all. The walls are only
frames for the sea. You get it from every window except
two on the moors. The effect is like out-of-doors, with
perfect ease and a fire to sit by and enjoy it. An invalid
might live shut up there for years and never miss the
feeling of open air. He says it is a house for winters as
well as summers, and the winters are dull down there."

"But he has Ralph Robbins and all the young
artists to help him; why does he tie himself to your
apron-strings?"

"They bully him, artfully. He stands a better
chance with me of getting his own way. That's where he
and I are in collusion."

"You are rather too much in collusion, if you'll
let me say so. Of course, it's very good-natured of
you—almost too good-natured; except" (I deliberated
and decided to go on) "that, since what happened

last summer, Tony has become a part of our lives and
I suppose we must learn to know him." Once more,
urged by an instinct that it was the right remedy
just now for my dear Cecy, I applied my dose of
unauthorized but unfaltering truth. I gave her the story
of Gareth and Lynette, from its original hopelessness,
the almost comical disparity, to the subtle drawing
together in their innocence of heart and love of beauty,
of those twain who were of one spiritual flesh. Then
the parting with sorrow to one of them—to both, as I
believed—down to the sudden sweep of Tony's fortunes
into the lime-light and Katherine's bewilderment. Her
last word I could not give; that was Tony's. I left it at
the interrogation mark.

Cecy listened, quite breathless; she changed
countenance; she flushed and paled and pulled herself
together gallantly. I think nothing but her vanity was
really hurt; that undoubtedly had suffered a sharp
pang, and she felt a little foolish, perhaps, as to the
"Dolly" theory. Suddenly she laughed.

"The simplest are the deepest. Has she given him
any hope?"

"That is not for me to say," I evaded brazenly.

"Well, I wonder if he is building that house for
her? He'd better look out; I wouldn't dare to build a
house for Katherine. But, of course, all the rest of it's as
plain as day. Poor Emilia Curtis! Now I see why all girls
look alike to him; he's practically a married man."

"Oh, very far from that, I should say. But every
man hopes to the last, so long as she isn't married."

"Hush, there he is!" As Cecy looked out of the window her color rose hotly, then she turned to me and smiled. She was safe, my much-tried girl; the slightest, frailest of our three, whom I had feared would not be equal to even such plain wifehood as my own. I count a good strong interest and pride in one's country, religious belief of some kind, the love of husband and children as the three great safeguards for a woman of thirty; Cecy had only one, her children. Peter had been a peril, never a safeguard; her love of country, like that of most of her generation who are not readers of history, was undeveloped; her religion, in the shyness and Unitarianism of my own bringing-up, I knew almost nothing about. She went to church, as a good Episcopalian now, with her little sons. But what she knew of God I had never asked nor hinted at asking. Her faith in that support was a thing I took on trust for what time she should go deep enough into experience and suffering to need it. Mine, I thought, had come when I lost my first baby: but there were good grounds for my shyness in these probings of another's heart. So, on the whole, I could say it was a victory for Cecy, in this trial we ourselves had brought upon her; the more dangerous because it had come to her so authorized, and in the guise of an upright man unsuspiciously her friend (and a fatal contrast to her husband).

In the course of her own sifting-out she had done a great deal, I could not deny, to help Tony range himself in a manner suited to his new fortunes and to his hopes of Katherine. Sitting at her feet he had listened to her social platitudes that he might be clothed on with that armor too, invulnerable at all points. Katherine would not care for the change in him, but its newness would wear off (as his shaved upper lip had recovered its color and mobility), and it was only a matter of externals, anyhow. She would not grudge him such support as he might find in it on the way to better grounds for self-confidence. Back in his Latin ancestry would be a love of dress, of forms and traditional etiquette. I adored Tony, but I never could help speculating about him as one of another species, which Charley would say proved him not "our kind of folks." But why not a better kind?

XVIII

Later by a day or two, Tony asked me if I would drive down to Vallevista with him some day, and meet the General at the new house. I said any day that he wished, when Cecy could go. And I turned to Cecy with the question.

"I've been twice," said she. "I think Tony wants just you and father this time."

"You know—I am very much afraid of your judgment, when it comes to putting houses on that shore," said Tony.

"You may well be," I assented; "but not because I have any judgment."

"Mamma has antipathies. She puts out her feelers and wiggles them and if she doesn't like, she draws them in and goes the other way."

"Not always! Tony knows that. I spent one whole summer with my feelers tucked in, and didn't go the

213

other way, and it was all on account of a house on the shore too."

"Yes," said Tony pensively. "Well, this isn't quite as bad as the hotel—not as big, anyhow."

He made the appointment by telephone that evening and called me up to say that the General would be able to meet us at Vallevista next day at noon, and we should lunch at the new house. My husband was then staying with Tony in the doctor's house, which they also used as a temporary office. It annoyed me somewhat that he seemed to be doing nothing toward our own housekeeping arrangements for the summer. Tony, he said, lived well; had a cook superintended by Aunt Luisa and between them the meals were "fine." This was all very well, but it really settled nothing. I had been with Cecy nearly a fortnight and her father had not been up once—too busy, he said. And as for the curtains—*my* curtains—I was quite sufficiently be-curtained in hearing so much about Tony's.

It was a beautiful drive. All impatience that I had felt or could feel with anybody I loved melted away in that sunshine about us, and any misapprehensions blew away on the sweet sea-wind. We entered Vallevista by the main street, but turned off into a side-street before we came to Mr. Hoadley's block, and in a moment we were stopping in front of the doctor's house in its shrubby little garden. The rose-climber had been trimmed and the garden showed care.

"Why is this fence down?" I asked, referring to the neighbor with the cat.

Tony said he had bought that lot to make a bigger garden and to get an entrance for a garage on the side-street. So things were happening already.

He went into the house and returned at once saying my husband had left word that he had been called down the shore by some scraper-teams in trouble; he might not be at the Point before four o'clock. This meant that we must lunch without him, which we did—at Tony's, Aunt Luisa joining us at short but beaming notice and delaying us with enchanting digressions of all kinds, especially the innocently boastful kind on her one theme.

At our old turn into the fields Tony slowed down and asked if I would like to drive out to the shore and look at the old camp-ground. "We can go on from there to the Point, though it's nearer this way; but we have plenty of time."

I said I did not care to see it: no ashes of deserted fires for me that day! It was so plainly the day of the future. From the hilltop as we climbed, we gained the whole coast-line, so well remembered, with its points ranging north and south as far as Pigeon Point Light. There should have been the hotel at a distance, stark and high against the west. But only the tank-tower stood up there alone.

"What's become of it? It's gone!" I cried.

"Wrecked," said Tony quietly. "All that was good for anything has been hauled away. You couldn't bear it, you said."

"But, mercy! You didn't take me in earnest?"

"I always took you in earnest. What is a hotel!"

"Well! I'm startlingly honored. But where is the blessed little garden? I hope you didn't wreck that too?"

"Never!" said Tony. "The watchman takes care of that. His house escaped, being small. He still watches campers,"—he smiled at me. "You look troubled. Have I really shocked you?"

"No; but I must remember you are the Djinn of All Deserts now. It won't do for me to be so careless in my talk. Have you really destroyed anything of value, money value?"

"Not a thing that I wanted to keep. It wasn't even well-built. Very likely it would have burned down some day, perhaps with people in it, if those old stovepipes had got too hot."

We were crossing the trestle over Bean Creek, on it, not under, as the old road went. A little farther and the two roads met, and we were bowling along in silence, when the Point came in sight stretched out lazily in profile, greener and more blossomy than I had ever seen it, with richer chromes and umber and lake in the colors of its rocks above the flashing lines of surf. A child's continent, a place of joyful and beautiful hopes where now it was full day. We old afternooners might pack up our dreams and our ghosts and glide out of sight, and leave youth its mornings and its future.

We drove in, not by the builders' road, deep-rutted and dusty, but making our own track through the sweet-smelling pasture. I shut my eyes to any sight, to any memory but those belonging to that day with

Katherine. And while I stared afar towards Cortez's rock, expecting to see something very grand up there built by Tony, lo, we were close upon the house itself through a gateway (where no gate was) into the very lap of the sweetest little garden-court walled in and waiting to be planted, smiling in sunshiny reveries of its loveliness to be.

"Oh, my!" I cried, as if I were alone. "Why, Tony, this is just where we meant to build."

"Where did you expect me to build?"

"Why, I thought you'd go up high for the bigger view."

"Because I lived in the hotel?" He laughed. "But this is the only place for a home. You said, I remember, that you couldn't live with all of your view in sight every moment of the day."

"Well, you had your own little walled garden; now you've got it *de luxe*. And you deserve it!"

Tony was very silent; he remained so all through our progress, traversing the rooms on the fair first floors—open-eyed, as Cecy had said, and clear—a house all lighted and voiced by the sea. We ascended to the half-floor, a sort of mezzanine that led to the drawing-room with long windows looking west (this room was unfurnished), and on and up to the exquisitely fitted bedrooms and baths which showed the fashionable architect's enlightened views and Cecy's little personal touches. It was charming to think she had done it all for Katherine, unconsciously, who would never have been so clever for herself.

"This is absolutely perfect," I said, as we wandered down again slowly, step by step, not to lose a single aspect or detail. "But I am haunted by a feeling that I've seen it all before. I've never been shown a single one of your plans, you know."

We returned to the library, down a short, low passage two steps below the entrance-hall. Here were the empty shelves, waiting as the garden waited, in a peaceful muse, for its occupants who would speak in the silent winter evenings by the fire.

"Now, come! What is the mystery of this house? Have I dreamed it? Why do I seem to have seen it all before? I *know* this room!—because I imagined just such a room myself."

"You did, and made a little sketch of it on an envelope I lent you—you don't remember. I've kept everything that belonged to last summer. I loved that house of yours. It hurt me when you said it never would be. And I made this house as much like it as I could, from what you said and the little sketches you used to make when you and—when you were talking."

"Sketches?—scrawls! You must have listened with a master mind to work up this out of anything I ever said. This is our house, only glorified. We couldn't have come within a thousand miles of it ourselves. We couldn't have had Ralph Robbins."

"He had the 'mind.' But I never told him whose ideas they were that I wanted him to work out. I couldn't talk about it, somehow. It was too much like building on the grave of your own home that you gave up so quietly. It isn't past!"

"Well, bless it for a lovely home, anyhow; and bless whoever lives in it! You are too dear to have done it so beautifully, so wonderfully. I am so happy to see how it has turned out. Not that we could have done it. How wonderful it is to be young. You can finish all the old folks' failures; you will realize our dreams and a great deal better ones."

"Oh, no!" said Tony, with a strange cry of sorrow in his tones. "Dream your dream once more, dear lady. This is your home, for many happy years, I hope. It was built for you and your good husband. This is the hacienda. Built for those who have seen so much and want so little. You taught me what a home is, whether a tent or—even a 'hotel,' or this—that I want you to love as if it were your own."

"Oh, Tony! must it be for others always that you build? Where is your house on the shore?"

"My house—?" He did not speak for a moment; he took my hand, my old, thin, bony hand, and raised it to his lips (the Latin in him). "My house is not on the shore. I think I could not bear the shore alone. When I want it I shall come down here to you. May I come very often?"

The gift of tears is not for the old; my eyes water easily, but I seldom weep. Not for years had I cried as I did then. It was not for anything he had said or meant to say, nor was it any one disappointment or shock or strain; it was the whole year that rolled in and broke upon my heart as Tony's heart was broken. I could not bear this last blow to him that finished my own hope too. There was no one for him to build for but us, the old ones—to coddle ourselves with books and bathrooms and flowers, and a view to show us how far it is to one daughter in the West that is East, and how far to the other in our East that is West to her. And another daughter lonely as Iseult of Brittany, waiting with her children for a stained, ignoble Tristram to wash his sins clean in the blood of holy wars. And Tony, with everything in his gift and nothing for himself! We had taken even his shore—Last summer he had been content with that. Now he could no longer bear it, alone.

"Has she never written to you since she went to France?" I asked him; I felt that I must make sure.

"Yes; once," he said, resignedly, as if some private verdict were always in his mind. "She said beautiful things—better than I can ever deserve. Did you know what I wrote to her? How I answered her letter?"

I said I had read his letter.

"I suppose I lost her then."

"No; no: she was proud of that. She glowed over it. Be at rest; you did not lose her then. Did she say nothing at all about—after the war?"

"She said: 'This is going to be a long war. You must not wait for anything. Live your life as fast as you can. If you could see how lives are going over here, you'd feel crazed to think of any one's waiting!'"

Should I tell him what she had meant to say?—before the whirlpool caught her and she had no more breath to spare? I dared not lay a finger more upon his life, my dear Tony. All I said was the trite thing we all were saying about the ones who go to France. The old life loses its reality; there can be no more belief in places like the shore. I told him how she had spoken once of "personal happiness" as a thing she no longer played with—"Let any one go in for it who can stand it." She has this work to do and she cannot dare to look back or dream dreams—or allow another to dream for her sake.

"There is plenty to do here," said Tony, not passively—even with a certain bitterness. "But it is harder than I could have believed it could be."

"How harder?" I asked.

"Of course I want to go where she is. But she would spot the 'personal happiness' there. No; as the General said, this is my 'front.' I must stay and try to work out every wish of hers that you can tell me about. I shall come down here to you and we will plan these things that she would want to see done. And the General will help me work the rest of the ranch so as to support them. And perhaps we may join this front on to hers over there."

"And where will you live, Tony? Have you thought about that at all?"

"Oh, yes; I have a house—the doctor's house. A better man than I shall ever be lived there very contented with his books and his work for company.

He spent his life for others, never thinking of any other life, and he never had what he wanted for himself—the one thing he knew that he never could have. And yet if you had seen him you would have taken him for a happy man."

XIX

All days are not days of prescience, but it was a haunted summer. Haunted by the nation's slowness, awful slowness; haunted by the dead of the Lusitania (their faces, living and dead, were in the New York papers lying casually on our tables); haunted by our trance-like inability to act, which ended in "screams of baffled rage"; haunted by our weird apathy in between; we were learning to accept anything. Friends in the East wrote passionately: "Will going to war mend it? Will killing more people bring those dead to life? If we take up the sword, who will be left to make peace?" American families were ashamed of their immunity, hence these tortured explanations. I was conscious of an unearned pride in our own small and involuntary share in the sum of sacrifice. It made it a little easier to write to a friend in England, mother of an only son at the front, that we had a daughter there—and a son-in-law! Poor Cecy was not ironical about Peter; she held up her head in these days and was proud to answer questions about him. He had taken what he called "a little fleet of wagons" across and was driving one of them and was his own mechanic—more of those glorious, blackened hands!

But the most silent and the most to be envied of us all was Tony. He looked no more at the door that would not open—to all "personal happiness" he had said adieu. We had many guests at the Point, our few and Tony's whom he shared with us, using a judicious thoughtfulness in selection. He enlarged his own house as we knew he would; hospitality was in his blood as well as tact. He began to take on a more expressed graciousness of manner added to his gentleness and quietude, which held in it a modest consciousness of power. There was a touch of the priest in Tony. When I said this to my husband he reminded me that once I had pronounced him the very stuff for a faultless trooper.

Among Tony's guests that we were to remember was a young French priest who was a soldier too, one who took last confessions in the trenches and went over the top as a brother to men he had shrived as their father in God. He had been fatally gassed (this was in the beginning of "chlorine warfare") and had not a year to live, but that did not hinder his coming to happy America with woes in his heart which it was his mission to tell—but you saw he never could tell half of what lay behind his tragic eyes and more tragic smile, to drawing-room audiences of jeweled women however kind.

This visit was to bear fruit, but the harvest is not yet and it does not belong in my story. That is Tony's story which cannot be written here without forestalling his plans and hurting his reluctance to pose as a benefactor. It will all come out in time. I wondered sometimes if in the end he might not find that he "wanted his mother's religion," as poor Maria had hoped. It certainly gives scope and imagery to that practical form of virgin motherhood which is one pure gift of these dreadful times. Old fat French nuns who could have worn the cross that is won on the field of honor, stooping their veiled heads beside modern young girls, free thinkers in every sense, both of them with Christ in their hearts, and their lives at the service of suffering.

Katherine was one of these nurses enforced by circumstances and election. She had had more training and rather more experience than most of the lay-nurses, but she had not expected to be assigned that work and would have hesitated to offer, deterred, perhaps, by current sarcasms about the "fevered brow" aspirants who had rushed in large numbers over to France. But that first crop of enthusiastic amateurs was giving out or being sifted out and many of the real ones had duties at home. There was the need, and, as she explained, they "take anything." The breaking-in we knew was ghastly. How she endured, I wondered, with her slender body and highly tempered nerves; but nerves are like faith, they continue their work when they have nothing to work with but the spirit and the will. They are the stuff of victory and she won her fight; she became inured in that extraordinary way—beaten hard and resilient like steel.

The war went on and the Notes went on. In one of Katherine's letters she said: "Read 'Battle Sleep,' Edith Wharton, in August Scrib. I know your ocean is as bare as it is safe, and you know there are no 'flame-seared lids' in my case. But, mams, that 'sail' that 'leans westward to the fading rose'—that's my word to you, my old steady longing for you and your blessed shore. I am there with you on your evening walks no less because I happen to be here. Are we down-hearted? Do we want to go home to our mothers? Well, rather! But all of us who can will see this to a finish; it would be a kind of suicide to end of our own choice what we know is the only life we shall dare to live while this keeps on."

I counted her rests; they were far apart and very short. If I could only have given her some of my superfluous rest, my solitude and silence in our corner of the world—

"Where quietly still the waves go out to sea
From the green fringes of a pastoral land."

Every sunset on the shore-path was our place of meeting, through that vision in her memory driven home in the poet's words. The shore hardly changes from mile to mile: eastward above the dusky moor-fields the slowly brightening quarter betokened moonrise on nights when there was a moon. The low-curtained twilight lifted in the west and showed the fading streak of rose. But not a sail; as bare as it was safe! Now and then we watched the smoke of a Pacific liner far in the offing and thought of her brightly lighted cabins and her passengers with nothing to fear. It was peace, but it was presage and the auguries were thickening in our path. I do not mean altogether those evil birds, the "sinkings," which were so constant the name for them had become slang. Nor our weary acceptance of note after note; my poor soldier flounced like one of his own hooked fish when he read them. And we knew that our friends who clung proudly to their white banners regarded us as male and female survivals of the age of force—"Prussianized Americans."

No; it was not the nation's plight nor the nation's warnings that haunted my wakeful nights altogether; but those secret, sudden strokes upon the heart, whispers of foreknowledge that send a shiver through one's veins. What matter if a girl, for instance, should cut off her hair!—if it saved her eight to ten minutes every morning dressing in the cold? Why cry about a bunch of fair hair? She was "losing such a lot of it, anyhow," she wrote, "and we are veiled most of the time. Even if I came home to be a bride like a good girl, there would still be the veil for my diminished head."

I wrote her despairingly: "I hope you didn't leave that hair I *loved* at the barber's! Send it to me. If there's any part of you that's detachable that you don't use and can't take care of, I want it back."

She replied with a wild jeer that she had nothing more left to detach but her teeth, which she really proposed to take care of and needed in her business. "I will send you my wig if you promise not to have a switch made of it, you old Victorian! It's queer I didn't leave it at the barber's; but I hall suspected he'd use it in *his* business, and I can't quite go the notion of some one else putting on my mortal remains while I am, generally speaking, still in the flesh. You can't deny it's classic to lay down one's virgin tresses, and you wouldn't mind a bit if it were only on the altar of Hymen!"

It came after a while, the wreath of hair coiled and pressed in a pasteboard box. The severed ends were tied hard and fast with one of Katherine's ribbons in one of Katherine's knots—I could see her doing it emphatically, to stay!—"There you are, mams; that's done!"—and packing it off in some spare moment.

I carefully straightened it out its full natural length, but it sprang back again in those enforced coils. Pale, soft, so tractable and fine, but with such a trained will of its own! As if nothing that had ever been a part of Katherine could lose its impetus and given direction. The hair seemed alive, sensate; I put it away with anguished tenderness.

Her last letter was written after Seicheprey, at the end of the second month of the German offensive. She said: "I am not allowed to tell you which sector the wounded come from, but they come in a staggering flood. So, my dears, don't talk to me of the time I've been away—the time is now. This is the decisive year."

It must have been immediately after this she had to give up with an attack of grippe. She had had it before, mildly; this time it was not mild; she got up too soon and died of the fatal relapse that follows an error or disobedience of this kind. With her it would have been inevitable. The deliberate suspension of her judgment; the giving way to that flaming will which drove her into excesses of work till she dropped. Her death, we say to each other, was not a mistake, it was a necessity of her previous life and her whole attitude toward life; and it was that in her which counted. She lost no time.... And now that she is gone there is no more to say about us as a family: Patty's story has scarcely begun; Cecy's pauses till Peter comes back; Tony is committed to his chosen work, and Katherine's work is done.

The chapter I had hoped to add, that would have rounded out her womanhood, will never be written. If we could have had her with us once more, *realizing how short the time must be*, we then might have given her back. Was she afraid? I have wondered!—afraid of Tony's longing? She had seen so much waste of youth and life and the hope of lives to be—did she fear that she might be tempted to give all while she had it in her power to grant one man his immortality of joys? A man may marry and go back, but a woman—

hardly! It is best to let things rest; but it grieves me to know there will never be wife or child for Tony. As he built for others and planted for others, so he will go on, sheltering the homeless, fathering the fatherless, comforting the lonely hearts, his own the loneliest of all. And the happiest, shall I say? In time I think he will be.

To go back to our own dreary selves, my old general asked nothing more after we were in the war but his orders. They separated us for long months; and this was unexpected, but he was given command of one of the new training-camps in a Southwestern State where nearly all the first summer was spent draining and sanitating the land; a fine job for that community the Government put through, at great expense and loss of time. Knowing my husband's opinion of politics mixed with patriotism and with army affairs, I could admire his silence; not one word of grousing in a single letter. But I! I love a grievance, at my worst; and during that time of unrest and feverish impatience I fear I was often at my worst. And then came Katherine's death and silenced even me.

I am here at the Point getting rooms ready for Patty and her little brood who will soon be home, with *two* babies now, and a Philippino nurse and a mountain of baggage. The transport has just left Guam. Her captain with his regiment has been ordered to Siberia. Patty will stay with me till more is known about the conditions for wives and babies at "Vlad.," as they already are slanging it. They write in the highest spirits eager to get into even that far fringe of the war. I have taken away the treasure of my heart, that wreath of hair, from the drawer where I hope Patty will put some of her baby-things; sweetness upon sweetness, life upon life. There is no death to me in not seeing my darling. Have I not gone years without seeing her?

Peter has got into the coveted Air Service; he is already an ace. This cannot have happened by accident or favor; they do not in Aviation waste time on anything in the nature of junk. Peter is winning the applause he so sorely craved and needed when he went to France. He writes to his wife and she believes in his better love and trusts he is as constant to his new professions when on leave as he has to be on duty. He is called, I hear, one of the miracles of the war. My opinion does not matter, but I reserve it, anyhow, till after the war is over and we have Peter home again, shorn of his wings. I agree that one life is as good as another to give in a great cause, but not to keep for when the cause is won and we have to live up to its aims and be true to the meaning of its sacrifices.

It was not enough for Katherine just to die, nursing dying soldiers; she should have nursed living children and helped Tony to broaden his life on the shore that meant work as well as peace and rest.

The End

About the Author

Mary Hallock Foote was born on November 19, 1847, near Milton, New York, where her Quaker family owned a farm. She studied art at Cooper Union in New York City and became a successful illustrator for *Harper's* and *Scribner's*. Her career as a writer and her Western experience began after her marriage in 1876 to Arthur De Wint Foote, a civil engineer from Connecticut. They were often apart, but she went with him to New Almaden, California; Leadville, Colorado; southern Idaho; and Grass Valley, California. She was one of the first women regionalists to write about the western part of the United States and she enjoyed an extensive career as a popular and well-reviewed author, publishing numerous essays, three collections of stories, and twelve novels from the 1880s into the 1920s, often illustrating them. In the 1920s Foote wrote an autobiography that was not published until 1972 titled *A Victorian Gentlewoman in the Far West: The Reminiscences of Mary Hallock Foote*. In 1932 the Footes retired to a daughter's home in Massachusetts. Arthur died the following year, and Mary survived him by five years, dying in 1938.